SHANNON JUMP

Like A Bird In Flight

First edition

ISBN: 979-8-218-00167-4

Editing by Librum Artis Editorial Services

This book was professionally typeset on Reedsy.
Find out more at reedsy.com

ALSO BY SHANNON JUMP

Contemporary Fiction

My Only Sunshine

Stand-Alone Psychological Suspense Thriller

Even Though it's Breaking

Crimes of Passion Series: Psychological Thriller

Wouldn't You Love to Love Her

Like a Bird in Flight

ADVANCED READERS COPY

The following is book 2 in the *Crimes of Passion* series and is not meant to be read as a stand-alone novel. Please ensure you've read the first in series, *Wouldn't You Love to Love Her* prior to continuing on with the series.

You have received an unedited proof copy. Any typos or errors should not be considered when preparing reviews. The author reserves the right to make additional changes prior to official publication without informing the reader.

Your spoiler-free reviews are greatly appreciated!

CONTENT DISCLAIMER

This book is intended for readers over the age of eighteen and contains mature content unsuitable for younger audiences. For a full list of warnings, please contact the author at info@shannonjumpwritesbooks.com.

For Vicki

I have no doubt the Shannon Jump collection
would have been front and center on your bookshelves.

A true *passion* that burns
within your soul
is one that can
never be put out.

~Zach Toelke

MY FORMER LIFE AS A PORN STAR

Alisha

I've imagined killing her at least a dozen different ways.

Not that I'm proud to admit that, but she deserves to be punished for what she's done. Some days it's all I can think about, her death, and how I'd do it, how I'd kill her.

The options are endless really. Up close and personal, a stranger-like attack, a random incident or accident. But nothing would be more satisfying than extinguishing her up close and personal.

Slow and steady.

Painful.

A kitchen knife, although messy, would certainly do the trick. It'd be fitting even, if not for the irony, considering she once used the same weapon to murder my husband, Dylan.

Got away with it, too, she did.

I imagine shooting her would feel pretty good too, but I don't own a gun and forensics can usually trace a bullet back to the gun that fired it, and therefore the shooter, anyway.

Too risky.

I suppose that part doesn't matter given my current predicament.

No, if I were to do it, I mean *really* do it, I'd probably drug her. The other options would be fun, sure, but they're too merciful, if not predictable.

Certainly way too easy.

I think I'd enjoy it a lot more if I were to go the drug route, maybe inject her with some paralytic drug, like Succinylcholine or Vecuronium, and render her muscles useless. She'd be fully conscious and alert, but immobilized. Defenseless. *That* would be gratifying, stimulating, maybe even empowering in some fucked up way. I'd be free to do whatever I want to her after that. I could take my time, savor the moment.

Choke her.

Smother her.

Torture her.

Honestly, with all the new "friends" I've made here at the Smithson Women's Penitentiary over the last year, it'd be easy to get my hands on whatever I'd need to do the job. A walk in the park, really. In here, everyone knows someone (who knows someone) who can get their hands on anything (or anyone) for the right price.

Fortunately for me, I have plenty of money to spare; I've saved millions thanks to my former life as a porn star.

I lay back in my bunk, sinking into the thin mattress that does little to separate me from the metal frame, and fold my arms behind my head as I stare at the ceiling. I have nothing but time in here. Time to think, time to daydream. For what this place lacks in comfort, it makes up for in that regard. Even as a bit of a loner, life on the outside was a constant ebb and flow, chaotic. Every day a never-ending list of to-dos without the time to actually *do* any of it. But here?

Here it's like a clock with no numbers, a series of light and dark, night and day.

An endless routine of monotony.

The mind has free reign to wander, to conjure.

I picture myself jamming a needle into the fatty meat of her arm, the injection quick, but effective. I'd watch as her eyes go wide, as she starts to feel the course of the drugs through her veins, as she loses control of her limbs. The side effects would kick in before she'd realize what's happening, that her life was about to end. That I was going to be the one to take it from her. I'd want her to know, of course. Revenge always tastes sweeter that way.

That's the beauty of it, you see?

I'd finally get to watch *her* suffer.

I've waited a long time for that.

Problem is, I'm a convicted murderer. So, despite this overwhelming desire to kill my former lover turned nemesis, Ivy Rogers, I'll be waiting a hell of a lot longer for *that* day to come. You knew that, though, didn't you? You couldn't possibly have forgotten all about my little situation, how I'm stuck in prison for a crime *she* committed. You probably even think I deserve to be here, and that's fine. That's your opinion, and you're entitled to it.

But you're wrong.

I suppose it *is* a little silly of me to daydream about killing someone on the outside when I'm stuck in here doing hard time, though. It's incredible how guilty an innocent person can look under the right lighting.

Shadows sure can be deceiving.

Not that I'm all that innocent anymore. There's still that other murder I *did* commit, the one I *am* responsible for, that's preventing me from living out this incredible fantasy. I'm not getting out of here any time soon, despite my wrongful conviction.

Doesn't mean a girl can't dream.

Still, everyone knows the incarcerated need something to look forward to when they get out. Something that drives us, entices us to roll out of these makeshift beds every day, to eat the food that tastes like cardboard and often smells like a toilet seat. There's usually an end goal—family, money, revenge. And when there isn't? Well, I'm sure you can figure out what happens to *those* inmates.

All hope is lost once a person loses their will in here.

This place is such a mind fuck.

CLUSTERFUCK

Alisha

If I could get my head to stop spinning, that'd be great. You know that feeling you get when you're about to pass out? How your hands get all tingly before they eventually go numb, followed by your feet, your legs. The next thing you know, you're hot all over, feverish, lethargic. Clammy, possibly even breaking a sweat.

The room becomes hazy.

The space around you caves in.

And you know—you just *know*—that you're about to go down, that you're headed straight to the ground and you're not about to take the fall gracefully either.

Drop and flop, more likely.

So classy.

The physical reactions are so similar to fear. And that's what I go through every single day, that's my life now. I feel like I'm about to pass out, only seconds away from the edge, at any given moment of any given day.

And I always eat shit.

I always land on my ass.

There's really no other way.

Three hundred seventy-two days. That's how long I've been here. It feels like an eternity already, but my time has only just begun. The days tick by in slow motion, the images of a past life fading one by one; soon they'll be gone entirely.

Forgotten.

Erased.

And I see the face of a complete stranger, remembering the moment she locked eyes with Judge Wyman and uttered the word "guilty" amongst a courtroom of spectators. She couldn't even make eye contact with me, couldn't bother to look *me* in the eye when she sealed my fate with that one single word. Almost as if she herself didn't believe the verdict that had been rendered.

I often wonder if she was the one juror who wasn't quite sure. Kyle Lanquist, my attorney, had said there was one, that they probably caved from the pressure, from the vindictive eyes of the eleven others, eventually.

Just one.

But if that's the case, if she *was* the one, she must not have felt too strongly one way or the other, because that jury was only out for three hours and twenty-six minutes. Certainly not long enough to decide the next twenty-five years of a person's life if you ask me.

The American judicial system at it's finest, my friends.

What a clusterfuck.

It replays in my mind daily, alongside snippets of Ivy—*Lila*—and Sawyer—*Grant.* But mostly I see images of Dylan. I see him smiling—*my husband*—laughing, loving me. I long to breathe him in, to smell his scent and feel the warmth of his body against my skin.

It almost seems unfair that he's gone.

But sometimes it feels like I deserve it, too. Like I'm *that* shitty of a human that the best I'll ever get from here on out is three mediocre meals a day, semi-clean prison scrubs, and a twice-daily orgasm at the direction of my own hand.

And now there's this letter.

Would you like to meet our son, Lisha?

My stomach turns as I read her words, not for the first time either. I've read this letter more times in the last couple weeks than I care to admit—the paper is worn from repeated folding and unfolding. But it still doesn't sit well with me.

How could it?

He looks a lot like his father, his namesake. I bet you'll appreciate that. I suppose I do, too. It's really too bad you had to go and get yourself convicted. If only you'd listened to me, Lisha...

She's been taunting me like this for months, sending letters just like this one—with just enough semblance of truth, but not enough for anyone but me to know—some with sonogram pictures, others with photos of her showing off her baby bump, updates on her prenatal appointments.

But this time it's a picture of him.

She's had a baby boy. Named after his father, and she's managed to rub it in my face—even from the outside.

My husband is the father of her son.

And I picture her there, smirking to herself as she writes these letters, her hand so heavy it bubbles the ink on the page as she writes. I take in the scribbled words on these crinkled pages, knowing she once touched them, and I soak them up like they're scripture to live by.

She played me.

Just like she played Dylan.

Just like she played Sawyer.

I see the irony in her words, in the accusations hidden within them, that all of this is somehow my fault. That I had it coming. She follows them blindly, accepts them like a brainwashed cult member or a child in church singing along to *Jesus Loves Me* and actually believing that he does. And it's fitting almost, her oblivion. Her lack of regard. It *has* to be, because I can't bear the thought of her knowingly being this conniving, this intentionally motivated.

I have to kill her.

Sometimes I think I humanize her too much, forgetting momentarily who she is, how capable she is of destruction. It helps to think about taking her life. She's already taken mine.

I need to get Dylan's son away from her.

But I don't know how to do that while I'm stuck in here.

Kyle was working on an appeal.

Key word: was.

He's not anymore.

The whole Shiv-Meets-Officer-Marshall's-Neck incident kind of blew that for me. That was my bad I guess. But, come on. That prick deserved it, and you know it as well as I do. He needed to be stopped, and I had no choice but to take that matter into my own hands.

I get why Kyle's pissed, I really do. I can't expect my attorney to work miracles. We had a chance—albeit a very small one—and now we don't. As if this is really a "we" thing and Kyle is actually affected, right? What a joke. Even if he could exonerate me of my husband's murder, it still wouldn't get me out of here. Not after what I've done.

There were new charges. For my actual crime, the one I *did* commit, and to say Kyle was unhappy to hear I'd taken the prison rape matters into my own hands would be an understatement. The man was truly livid, more so than I've ever seen him.

But what was I supposed to do? No one else would have done anything about it, and I was stuck here, merciless to the man. He stuck his claws in and refused to let go. And me? I was never getting out of here; I had nothing to lose and a chance to prove myself to the only people left who mattered.

My fellow inmates.

Or so I thought.

Now, with two very public murders on my rap sheet, I'm probably (definitely) stuck here for life, likely without parole or the ability to pass *Go*, which means my intentions of avenging my husband's death and taking out Ivy Rogers may never see the light of day. It almost makes me wish Minnesota were a death penalty state.

Some days I can't bear to soak in the misery buried within these walls.

Some days I just want it all to end.

But for now, I dream.

I plot.

I spend the core hours of my days suspended in time, locked in an eight-by-six cell with a woman who talks to herself and considers masturbation a sin. Whoever assigns cell mates in this place must've had it out for me.

There isn't much reprieve outside of lockdown hours either. Tiffany still has me wrapped around her bony little finger, but I'm forever indebted to her whether I like it or not. And desperate times called for desperate measures, so it is what it is.

At least no one bothers me anymore, no one catcalls or corners me in hallways and shoves their hand down my pants. There are always consequences for those who do, now that I've shown my true colors, now that Tiffany had made it clear who's hiding the shiv, and that's more than I can say for most of the women in here. At least I was resourceful enough to come up with a contingency plan; I knew what I was getting into.

But this fucking letter.

Ugh.

My husband has a son.

And *she's* his mother.

She'll get what's coming to her, though.

She *has* to.

Right?

COUPLE SEEKING FEMALE COMPANIONSHIP

PLAY THE VICTIM

Ivy

She wants to kill me.

I know it, and you know it. Sure, maybe one day that'll work out for her, who knows? For now, I wake up every morning and revel in the fact that she's locked up and I'm not. She can't touch me from where she's at. She doesn't have the connections she thinks she does, despite her wealth. Nobody even likes her enough to help her.

Her, being Alisha Thompson, federal inmate; local public enemy and envy of soccer moms everywhere.

It's my fault she's there, in that prison, I admit it, but that's beside the point.

She thinks she's the victim here, but she's not. No, *I'm* the real victim. She hurt me first. And an eye for an eye goes a long way when the trip itself is just a short jaunt.

Trust me, she got what she deserved.

Do I feel bad for what I've done to her? No, not really. She left me, so there was nothing more for me to lose. And Dylan? Ex-boyfriend of mine or not, it wasn't like there was any love left between us. That ship had long since sailed, and the animosity from him was getting a little old if you ask me. He took her from me.

So, no, I don't feel bad for what I've done.

This way works for me.

This way, we play by *my* rules. I set the tone, run the show, write the script; however you want to say it. Dylan's out of the way now, and Alisha can only run so far with her ankles chained together.

I haven't been by to see her yet, in the prison. Not for lack of trying; she simply refuses to see me. But she will. One day I'll take up residence at the top of her—very short, if not otherwise non-existent—visitors list. She'd be a fool not to want to meet her husband's son, and I'm the only one who could make that happen for her.

One phone call.

That's all she's given me in the time we've spent apart. Over a year now, and that's all I get. I'm sick of the cold shoulder act she's playing.

The boy will change all that eventually though, he has to.

He really is a cute kid; looks a lot like his dad. Nothing like *her*. Which is a shame. But he's *our* son, despite her lack of contribution to his DNA. And he may have been conceived out of spite with her now-dead husband against his will—although, he sure seemed into it until he saw the blade of the knife that killed him—but the boy's purpose has always been medicinal. He'll fix us, he has to. That baby is the one good card I have left in my hand.

And I intend to use it.

Did I intend for Alisha to get pegged for Dylan's murder? Not really. That was a bit of an accident.

Oops.

I simply wanted the man dead, out of her life.

Out of my way.

And I wanted *her* to suffer because of it, to feel his loss the same way I've felt hers since the moment she walked away without so much as a glance over her shoulder. I suppose that's where my little plan went a wee-bit south; I didn't quite think that part through, and that's on me. See, I wanted to catch her after her run, we'd pack a bag, grab some of her hard-earned cash, and off we'd go. But she came back early, while I was busy hiding evidence in a rented car down the street, and I didn't get a chance to explain. And that nosy neighbor of hers just *had* to go and call the cops—being the *concerned citizen* that she was.

She heard Alisha's screams, after all.

Not that her testimony in court was all that damaging in the long run. Alisha kind of hammered the final nail herself if I'm being honest.

Everything just happened so fast—a true crime of passion, if you will. Although, something tells me Alisha would disagree with that logic; she prefers to save passion for the bedroom.

Trust me, I know.

What I didn't know, was that she would come home early. That she'd walk right into that bedroom, pull the knife from her dead husband's torso, and hold it in her dominant hand while she stared down at his lifeless corpse. One may have even expected her to cry, but nope. She couldn't be bothered to do that either, because the woman was about as emotionless as yours truly. That's part of the reason we were so good together, not that it helped her in court.

And everything would have been okay if she would've just listened to me. We had time, we had means. Everything would have been fucking fine if she'd have kept her cool.

If it wasn't for that piercing scream.

I almost went back in there, you know; I wasn't planning to leave the murder weapon behind. I just hadn't gotten to it is all. But that scream changed everything.

That scream stole minutes from us, and now years.

It was silly of me to assume she'd be able to get herself out of it once the cops showed up, but I did, I made that assumption. I thought they'd know right away, that they'd see a distraught housewife and rush out the door in search of her husband's killer; the man was still warm for Christ's sake. They *had* to know she didn't do it, right?

Oh, how wrong I was.

Good thing I used gloves; fingerprint evidence sure would have been tough to explain. Without it, they had nothing.

And she was dead in the water, floating like a buoy without so much as an anchor to tie her down. I tried to tell her, to show her, that I'd be there for her. That with just a little more planning, I'd get her out of the mess she'd gotten herself into.

But she denied me. Wouldn't let me see her while she was in county lock up, wouldn't take my calls. And then, of course, completely lost her shit when I showed up at the trial to testify. As if she hadn't expected me to be there.

The initial plan was to lie.

To muck up the prosecution's case and make sure that incompetent lawyer of hers got the acquittal. But she fainted as soon as she saw me. Dropped right to the floor like a bird in flight shot down from the sky. There were simply too many witnesses by that point; she was a lost cause.

I had no choice.

Her reaction had given away the fact that we knew each other, that we weren't the virtual strangers I was otherwise happy to portray on her behalf—nothing more than sisters-in-law who had never met due to the tumultuous relationship of the brothers we'd chosen to marry.

And she ruined it.

At that point, I did the only thing I could think to do—I looked out for myself. Me, Myself, and Ivy. The only reliable trio I've ever known.

She gave me no choice but to revert to Plan B, to play the victim.

If Alisha managed to put two and two together after that, at least there was a good chance no one would believe her when she spilled her guts. I'd be free to go, and she'd be hauled off to prison for my crime. So, I showed that jury of our peers how Alisha's desire to play house with my husband and me did nothing but ruin my once-loving marriage—as if it remotely resembled that. My husband left me, he'd fallen for our mistress. So sad.

Poor Ivy.

As much as it pains me, it was incredibly easy portraying her as the sex vixen, as the home-wrecking whore who stole my husband. The DA liked to think—and he didn't hesitate to share this scenario in his closing statement—that Alisha had probably found out about her husband's affair with his ex-girlfriend—*me*—causing her to lash out, and thus murdering him in a heated crime of passion.

And let's be real, that's exactly what it looked like.

Of course, I made sure to leave out the part about the ménage à trois being *my* idea in the first place, and that I'd fallen deeply in love with her. We both did, my husband and I.

How unexpected *that* was.

I did my best to paint her as a flawed character and hoped each and every one of the jury members would see straight through her.

And they did.

She was the wife scorned, the porn star turned housewife. It wasn't a pretty picture, no matter how you colored it.

Nor was it hard to convince them; they'd all seen her work. They saw the nude pictures of her, the videos, and even Dylan's dead body all mangled and rotting on the marital bed they once shared.

The evidence really doesn't lie, does it?

Poor Alisha.

FUCKED UP-NESS

Ivy

I suppose it would only be fair for me to share my side of the story now. Alisha did get to tell hers, after all. You probably didn't even believe her at first—when she told you she didn't kill her husband—did you? I can't say I blame you; outwardly, she really *was* the likely choice. But how many times have you been told not to judge a book by its cover, hmm?

Tsk. Tsk.

You should have known better.

And yet, here you are again, doing the same thing to me. You don't even know me. I'm sure you think you do, but really, all you know about me is what you think you've learned from Alisha. See, so you're biased. We can fix that, you and I.

Before you go making the rest of your assumptions, let's back up. Let's make sure you have all the facts so you can make that informed decision you're so desperate to make.

First things first.

There's a common misconception that all fucked up people come from tragedy. That somewhere within their history lies a disturbance; signs of abuse, abandonment, addiction, mental health. The list goes on.

I, however, come from none of these things.

And I'm pretty fucked up.

Which means, it was probably the opposite in my case, right? My parents must have loved me *too* much. They must have put way too much of their energy into my education, extra circulars, and generally hovered like a helicopter over the scene of an accident, thus creating a narcissistic, entitled monster. Was *that* the thing that broke me?

Nope.

That wasn't it either.

I happen to come from a family of middle-class Americans—a working mother *and* father, a younger sister, Erika, who for the most part, annoyed me no more—or less—than the expected amount. My dad even wrote the occasional bounced check on pizza night because for some reason, he felt his family deserved delivery pizza even though he couldn't afford to pay for it.

What a guy, huh?

We lived in a three-bedroom, split-level home in a cul-de-sac on Rich Street in suburban Minnesota—and yes, we recognized the irony of this. There was a family dog (Stanley), two goldfish (Gil and Bob), *Monopoly* nights, snowball fights, and church on Sundays: the whole shebang.

Daddy didn't abuse me, Mommy didn't have a drinking problem, and Erika didn't make out with any of my boyfriends under the bleachers at the homecoming game. She never accidentally shrank any of my favorite sweaters in the wash or stole my CDs never to give them back either.

See, so there was nothing abnormal about my upbringing that would explain why I'm such a shitty adult. My husband, Sawyer—well, soon to be *ex-husband,* actually, if the papers ever show up—was determined to solve the mystery of *why Ivy is the way she is,* and even vowed to pay whoever he needed to ensure I "got over" my unexplained mental health issues. His words, not mine.

The thing is, I wasn't depressed, and I didn't have some diagnosable *thing* that could be treated with a regimen of pills and twice-weekly therapy. I tried to tell him this, but he's never been the greatest listener. Not to mention, his desire to fix me was outweighed by his inability to actually give a shit. I was nothing more to him than a wet hole to fuck and a piece of suckable candy to put on his tongue whenever the craving so hit him.

Too harsh?

Meh. It's fine, really. I was happy to play the part. It's not like I didn't benefit greatly from our arrangement.

But I'd be curious what the shrinks would have to say about me if given the chance; I do imagine they'd consider me an interesting case study. It doesn't make sense, this *anomaly.* Not statistically speaking, anyway. Scientists love data, they live for it. But my numbers are skewed; they're the outliers in what is otherwise an expected result.

I'm a motherfucking phenomenon—*yay me!*

At some point, I simply came to terms with the fact that I'm not like everyone else. Why I happened to be the apple that fell so far from the tree is beyond me.

All this to say, I'm well aware that *something* is off in my head. Do I care? Not really. I live life on my own terms, always have, always will. If you ask me, my fucked up-ness is my most endearing quality.

The way I see it? The fact that I'm broken doesn't need to be justified by reason; I just *am.* I do find it interesting though, and thought you might too. Again, trying to give you all the facts here. Does this understanding change my day-to-day? Make me more compassionate for others? More self-aware?

No.

In fact, I may lack compassion almost entirely, and I have seemingly zero tolerance for liars, for betrayers. That's why I live for vindication and revenge.

And I always come for it.

Always.

[LACK OF] PARENTING SKILLS

Ivy

I smell toast.

The semi-pleasurable, almost intolerable, distinct scent of burnt breadcrumbs in the bottom of a toaster waft into my nostrils as I come to. I'm also certain someone is pounding on the door, but when I roll over, I realize it's just in my head. I squint, and try to make out the time with a one-eye-opened peek at the bedside clock before remembering I no longer have a bedside clock. Everything is all about the smartphone now, you know. Only old people use digital alarm clocks, and I'm certainly not one of those.

At this realization, the day of my thirty-fifth birthday—yesterday—you better believe I promptly stripped my own digital clock from the wall and permanently relocated it to the garbage bin.

The things we do to stay young.

I'm having a bit of a hard time accepting my birthday this year. I know, I know, it happens to the best of us. But it's not supposed to be *my* time yet. I'm not supposed to be turning thirty-five, on the cusp of divorce, and still leaking from my tits.

Yet, I am.

Lucky me.

When I finally roll out of bed, I pad down the stairs, somehow drawn toward the sound of baby coos and Teflon pans. Why anyone would require a frying pan to prepare breakfast for a newborn is beyond me, but I suppose that's what I pay her for. She knows best, of course.

She, being my new nanny, Caramie.

She's been a godsend, and it's only her second week here. While I can't say I'm a fan of pushing eight-pound babies out of my vagina, it turns out I'm not much of a parent either. But, come on, are you really surprised?

Seven days.

That's about how long I lasted on my own before enlisting the full-time assistance of a nanny. Yeah, yeah, I get it—you're over there scoffing at my selfishness, ready to point your pretentious fingers in my direction and tell me to suck it the fuck up and start taking proper care of my child.

To that, I say *no thanks.*

That's why Caramie is here.

If you think about it, her presence is really in my son's best interest. He's better off with her, trust me. So, let's go ahead and get over your disapproval of my [lack of] parenting skills, okay?

Besides, I have other shit to do.

I see the kid every morning—as long as I manage to crawl out of bed in time to pat him on the head before Cara takes him to do whatever the hell they do every day—and again in the evenings if I make it home before his bedtime, which if I'm being honest, I tend to overlook. I have a hard time remembering what time the little guy goes down, and it's not like I have some sort of biological clock to remind me either. My milk is drying up and he's been feeding from a bottle for weeks now. If I see him, I see him.

And when I don't, Cara has it covered. What does she need me for?

Her presence has been great, though; she's a life saver, and I'm kinda patting myself on the back for hiring her. And not just because she takes care of the kid. She's on top of the household chores, too. Before her, I had a housekeeper, yes, but Sawyer had hired her years ago and the woman was a bit of an eye sore. I took the opportunity to class up the place a bit while I was at it.

Two birds, one stone.

Voilà!

What I *am* struggling with, aside from the dreaded birthday I just experienced, are two things:

1. Alisha is still in prison, and as you know, it's sort of my fault she's there in the first place.
2. Caramie is hot...like, *really* hot. (And, okay, fine, there's one more problem I need to take care of.)
3. Sawyer.

The only other person on the face of this earth with any inkling as to what really happened to his stepbrother, slash my ex-boyfriend, slash former lover's husband (it's complicated, I know. Don't worry, I remembered to update my relationship status on Facebook).

Let's chat about problem number one, shall we? Alisha.

I still think of her at night. I hear her voice, smell the lavender scent of her shampoo, and find myself longing for the softness of her touch, her kiss.

To taste her.

And that's confusing, because, well—feelings. I hate feelings. They suck, and I don't have time for them. That's what was so great about Sawyer (see problem number three above). The man was a steel vessel in human form. The only emotion he had was arousal, and is that even an emotion?

Probably not.

But he had it.

Insert problem number two: Caramie. What to say about her, huh? I found her on one of those nanny websites—and I don't mean the ones you go to after hours to find anything *but* an actual nanny. No, this was a reputable website where families in search of nannies can put in a bid in hopes that the nanny of their choice will agree to an interview in their home. There was a pamphlet on my bedside table at the hospital, and I happened to grab it *just in case.*

Did I intend to hire the first nanny I interviewed? No. And to tell you the truth, she was probably a little under-qualified for the job, being that I needed her to moonlight as a housekeeper, and the only thing on her resume was reception-related. Did I hire her anyway?

Yep, sure did.

She was easy on the eyes, what can I say?

"Good morning, Mrs. Rogers," Caramie says when I round the corner into the kitchen. She's wearing Sawyer's *kiss the chef* apron over her pajamas, stirring oatmeal on the stove while my son sleeps strapped in a bouncer on the island counter top. She simultaneously stirs the oatmeal while rocking him with her other hand, and I can't help but wonder what made her think to do that.

It seems almost...ingenious, and I chide myself for not having thought it before she was around. The baby even looks happy, unlike the mornings he and I were on our own and all he did was scream his face off.

"Caramie, I've told you, it's Ivy. Please. When you say 'Mrs' it just makes me sound old."

"Got it, sorry! Anyway," she says cheerfully, reaching in the cupboard for a bowl. "Is there anything you need from the grocery store? Dyl and I will be running errands today."

"Dyl?"

"Dylan, sorry," she corrects herself, patting my son on the head.

"Right. If you don't mind, let's not make *Dyl* a thing, okay? He wasn't named after a pickle."

She laughs, her button nose wrinkling in a way I'd rather not admit is adorable. But it is. And suddenly I can't help but think of myself as a cougar; I'm ten whole years older than her.

"You're not a pickle, are you, Mr. Dylan?" she says to my son.

And yes, I *did* name him after my former lover's deceased husband in hopes that she would see that as a sign that we are meant to be together and the so-called legacy of the child's father will live on.

It was a peace offering, what can I say?

I sit and watch Caramie for a moment, grateful she recently moved in full time. I'm in awe of how gracefully she moves around the kitchen. Everything seems like second nature to her. She slides a bowl of maple oatmeal to me, the spoon clanking on the side of the dish. I pull it out and set it aside to cool, placing my elbows on the marble countertop and making a steeple with my fingers.

"How are your accommodations? Are you comfortable in your room? Have everything you need?"

"Oh, yes! It's great, Ivy, I honestly can't thank you enough."

I'm sure I can find a way for you to thank me.

When the thought creeps into my mind, I stifle it and decide to grab a cup of tea and take it upstairs with my oatmeal. I need to behave—at least for a little bit. I can't afford to lose Caramie so soon, and I have a feeling hitting on her—at least without Sawyer's appendage hanging around—won't do me any favors.

Something tells me this one likes the dick.

"Good. Well, I'll leave you to it," I say. "Can you stop for the dry cleaning while you're out?" I hand her the slip from the refrigerator, too embarrassed to acknowledge the spark I feel when our fingers touch.

"Sure thing," she chimes.

Back in my room, I forego the oatmeal and reach for my vibrator instead. Hungover or not, I need to get the nanny off my mind.

The last thing I need is another crush.

PSYCHOTIC WOMEN FOR THE WIN

Sawyer

Psychotic women turn me on.

What can I say?

Ivy's crazy was the fuel that kept my fire burning. And she knew it. She was well aware of the power she possessed over me. She thrived on it, and went out of her way to remind me how quickly it could be taken away.

See, that's what you probably failed to realize before; I didn't leave Ivy. *She* left *me.* For *her.* Alisha Thompson, the former star of *Lisha's Bedroom* and object of our affection. I believe you've met, yes?

She's the one who changed Ivy, the reason our marriage failed.

Okay, fine, I *was* technically the one who walked away, but Ivy had already checked out, so can you blame me? I knew where things were headed and wasn't about to get caught up in the cross hairs.

I'm no idiot.

Now, I don't know about you, but I watched that entire trial play out. I consumed every second of media coverage, every day for weeks. I saw the way Alisha reacted when Ivy took the stand, the shock on her face when she realized her name wasn't Lila, the name we'd agreed to give her all those months before. You can't fake a reaction like that.

Ivy wasn't who Alisha thought she was.

And neither was I.

But that was by design, the way it was supposed to be. That anonymity was crucial, it shouldn't have surprised anyone, especially Alisha.

I considered coming forward, taking the stand and telling my side of the story. Part of me wanted to come clean to those twelve jurors, to the judge, and that lawyer of hers—who very clearly had a thing for her, let's be honest—and everyone out there watching that trial on television with the same level of interest that I had.

But I didn't.

Ivy would have had my balls in a sling.

She would've killed me.

I know it, and you know it. That woman would have ended me the same way she ended my stepbrother. Seventeen stab wounds to the chest? No fucking thank you. Sorry, brother, but I'd rather not take my chances.

I suspected it was her the moment I found out about my brother's untimely death. Murdering her ex-lover, the husband of the woman she loved but couldn't have? That was right up Ivy's alley.

So yeah, I ran. Like a damn coward, I stuffed my tail between my legs, packed my shit, and left in the middle in the afternoon while Ivy was off spending my hard-earned money on baby furniture.

I don't regret it, and no, I'm not the least bit ashamed.

Do I feel bad for Alisha? Guilty that she's off rotting in some prison for a crime that, let's face it, we all know she didn't commit? I mean, sure. I did have have a chance to stop it, and selfishly, I wanted her for myself just as much as Ivy did. Just as much as Dylan did. Alisha was the epicenter of our hurricane, and I think it's safe to say the three of us were nothing more than debris left behind after the storm cleared.

But let me tell you...it wasn't always this bad.

Ivy and Alisha were each crazy in their own way, yes, but it didn't start out that way. In the beginning it worked, just the right amount of crazy.

And what's better than one crazy woman in your bed?

Two.

I just never expected things to turn out the way they did.

DICK, MEET VAGINA

Ivy

I have an addiction.

Well, several, if I'm to be fully transparent, but we'll focus on just the two for now: sex and booze.

The extent of my sexual desires, my first self-diagnosed addiction, is not as severe as I imagine Alisha's was, but it's there nonetheless. The booze came after I lost her, then again once the baby was born and Sawyer moved out.

I suppose that's to be expected. We all have our vices, and after a breakup—hell, *two* simultaneously in my case, if you think about it—sometimes we need a little assistance in the coping department.

Sometimes we need a stronger vice.

Like sex.

And booze.

So, that's the current state of my life. Orgasms and drunkenness. If it helps, I do think of myself as high-functioning in both regards, but I suppose you'll establish your own opinion.

So be it.

Really, the booze is a buffer. It helps me feel better about all the sex, masks the variants of guilt that linger in the back of my mind every time I spread my legs to a new stranger.

And the brothels, which I may have forgotten to mention? Well, those simply feed both addictions. The vice is no longer just sex, or booze, it's the thrill of what could happen when the two mix together. The calculated risk, so to speak.

I crave it.

Need it.

Want it.

So I take it, every chance I get, I take from others to benefit my own desires, my own narcissism. I blame my husband—not simply because he chose to leave. Not because I'm lonely (I am) or to make him jealous (I'd love to).

But because he made this way.

He turned me into this.

Lila and Grant—*remember them?*—stemmed from that evil genius's mind. And I have to admit, I was all for it. The personas presented an opportunity; a general desire to spice things up in the bedroom. Sawyer and I were...adventurous, if you will, when it came to sex. The spice had been there from day one. Really, it never left, we just got bored, sex was too predictable.

We needed a hotter sauce.

We had sex so often that eventually it was the same old 'Dick, meet Vagina' saga. The routine just wasn't cutting it anymore; it was like our sex organs knew what to expect and suddenly wanted nothing to do with each other. And don't get me wrong—we tried. We got creative—handcuffs, role play, sex in public. Then, the dominatrix phase, which, I'll admit, was my favorite.

Each 'new' thing was great until it wasn't. We were a once and done couple, to no fault of our own. But the driving force in our marriage was sex, so what choice did we have but to work out the kinks?

Without it we had nothing.

The swinger's club was Sawyer's idea.

Because, yes, we went down that road, too. Of course, he'll deny it if asked. That's what the man does. Always claims to be so innocent when he's most often the instigator. And he gets away with it, too. A handsome man like that? Wealthy, emotionally unattached, smooth talker. Yeah, he's a real sweetheart.

"Don't take this the wrong way," Sawyer had said after a year of frustration. The tentative prequel to the act that would follow did nothing but set me up to do exactly that—take it the wrong way. "...but what if we try an open marriage?"

I couldn't conjure up an immediate response, so he continued under the assumption that my interest was piqued by the suggestion, when really, I was still a little hungover from our night out the prior evening. It took a few minutes to digest what he'd suggested, and in the mean time, he just kept talking.

"There are these events we could try," he said. "Swingers parties, brothels, wife swaps. That sort of thing."

"Isn't *Wife Swap* that reality show where the wives switch houses and have to take care of each other's unruly kids and clean their dirty toilets?"

He smiled, more so for my benefit than to confirm actual amusement. "No, Ivy—I mean, yes, it is, but you're getting off track. I'm not talking about a reality show."

"I know..." I shrugged, the need to explain suddenly lost on me.

"Okay, so..." he continued expectantly, as if my delayed response might send him into respiratory duress should I continue to withhold an opinion. "What do you think?"

I paused before throwing back the covers and climbing out of bed. "I *think* I have a headache," I said, sauntering off toward the bathroom to take a hot shower.

"Ivy..."

"Sure, whatever you think is best, Sawyer. Sign us up for the bake sale while you're at it, too," I replied flippantly.

"If you don't want to do it, just say so," he barked. I'd irked him.

Oops.

I stopped in the doorway, my arm draped along the trim, and looked at my husband. His hopes were up, I could see it. The need to try this one last thing prevailing over all else. "Do I get fucked?"

"Huh?"

"At these parties. Will there be dick and do I get to play with them?"

"Jesus, Ivy," he said, scoffing at my bold response. But his eyes were hungry, I could see it. The thought of someone else boning his wife turned him on. It always had, and I'd known all along.

"Well?"

"Yes. You can have all the dick your horny little heart desires, Ivy," he confirmed, a grin on his lips as he followed me into the bathroom. I winked and pulled my T-shirt over my head, dropping it to the floor.

"Then let's do it," I agreed before stepping into the shower.

Sawyer stripped and followed, wasting no time showing me just how grateful he was that he'd married such a compliant woman.

***

"So, how does this whole thing work?" I asked later that evening. I'd been making a mental to-do list all day, taking account of everything I'd need to prepare for our new adventure. Get waxed, a Brazilian, a massage to loosen my muscles, probably even a facial. I'd need to shop for some new lingerie too, of course, maybe some new heels.

"The swingers club?" he asked, doing little to hide the excitement in his eyes. "I think we just show up. There's an initiation process of sorts so we just watch at first. We can play with each other, but no other members until we're officially invited in. There are rules."

He's already done his research.

I nodded, increasingly more titillated with the idea.

"We can come up with fake names, too. Think of it as an acting gig or something, I don't know," Sawyer suggested. I shrugged.

"If you think it'll help."

"Who should I be?" he asked, and of course he would put the assignment on me. Picking fake names for a sex club? How hard could it be? Pretty people get fucked all the time, it doesn't matter what their name is.

"You be Grant, I'll be Lila," I said firmly.

And that was it.

Fuck if I know where the names came from. It didn't matter anyway; we were in agreement. Sawyer had been given his queue to sign us up for a revolving door of sexual partners.

I may have been complacent in my agreement at first, but I suddenly couldn't wait to get started.

SOCIAL NORMS

Ivy

Despite our well-thought-out plans and new names, Sawyer and I didn't *look* like the kind of couple to frequent a brothel, or any swingers club for that matter. Not that there's a certain *look* per se, but I'm sure you know what I mean. We were clean cut, reserved to the naked eye, but far from it if I'm being honest.

And that was the beauty of it; that elicited anonymity was crucial, something we both needed. There's a time and place to look the part and we pulled it off well, Sawyer especially. The man has that soft-spoken-nice-guy kinda thing about him that every woman and gay man fantasizes over.

We were different people once we set foot through those doors, all social norms went out the window.

These events aren't well-received by the general public, the average Jane or John Doe would disapprove at the very thought of walking through those doors, let alone give the opportunity serious consideration.

It's certainly not traditional to share your spouse with a third party.

But that's kind of what made it special, too. We had each other, but there was a certain pull that came from watching my husband fuck another woman. He said the same of watching me, too.

Unlike everything else we'd tried before it, group sex wasn't something either of us had the willpower to quit.

Not that I expect you to understand; I'm sure you're over there rolling your eyes, and that's fine. You'd have to experience it to understand it. People are judgmental by nature, always sticking their noses where they don't belong, giving unsolicited opinions, unwarranted advice. They can't help it, it's just what they do. How is our sex life anyone's business but ours?

We made sure it wasn't, that it stayed private at all costs.

Sawyer's job—our livelihood—depended on it.

His social circle has always been expansive, definitely more so than mine. More lucrative, too. That's what happens when you're a likable human. From clients, to investors, partners at the firm, any minor acquaintance really, and Sawyer immediately turns into a people-pleaser. He schmoozes with the wealthy leaders of the finance industry most often, desperate to stick a hand into their deep pockets and come out with a little extra for himself. But I'm sure he'll tell you all about his little side hustle, so I'll leave him to it.

Meanwhile, we played it cool, we acted the part, demonstrated the role of a *normal* couple. We were always good at that: role playing.

It's easy to show people what they want to see.

We're a good looking, wealthy couple with a lust for life, success, to be well liked in the community. At least, that's what our social media presence made it seem.

And the internet doesn't lie, does it?

But my husband's dark secret, his closed-door guilty pleasure, will make its way into the light soon.

I'll make sure of it.

A WORLD-CLASS IDIOT

Sawyer

Look, I didn't think she'd go for it, okay?

I didn't.

But I wanted to get into that club, and figured it wouldn't hurt to ask. And I didn't do it just for me, either, I did it for *her*. For us. I'm sure she's told you otherwise? Maybe even on the verge of convincing you that *I'm* the sex-crazed lunatic of this story?

Fine.

Whatever.

I'll step into those shoes and wear them like a man if that's what it takes. But know this: Ivy is one hell of an actress. The woman spent the first half of her life in community theater. That's how I found her, you know. Well, actually that's how my stepbrother, Dylan found her. I guess I can't take claim to that one since she wasn't officially mine until a good year later.

I'm just saying, don't believe everything that comes out of that woman's mouth. I may still be married to her on paper, but that doesn't mean I'd take a dip in the pool again any time soon, if you know what I mean.

The acting thing never did go her way. I suppose that's

why she goes so far out of her way to fuck with people in the real world. It's like a challenge for her, playing a character. When Dylan met her, she was the lead in some musical. One of those ones everybody knows the name of and has all the cheesy songs memorized and stuck in their heads for days. Not me. I can't stand those productions. Which is probably why I can't remember what the show was called to begin with.

Either way, she was an actress. Lead role in the play. Dylan had a pair of tickets some homeowner had gifted to him—perks of being a Realtor, I suppose—and he took Mom to the show, well, *his* mom. My stepmother. Dad and I respectfully sat that one out and played nine holes at Bunkers instead.

But Dylan had this knack for locking down unobtainable women. First it was Ivy, then when that went south for him, Alisha. I don't know how he did it, but apparently I made a habit of going after the same women for sloppy seconds. We've shared at least two in this lifetime, and I imagine that number would have gone up if he were still around.

My brother was a world-class idiot, though.

He chose work over Ivy. All the time, every time. Sure, he was trying to make a name for himself, get some cash in the bank. And Lord knows Ivy needed a man with financial means. She's a bit of a spender, that one.

It was the weekend of his first big commission; he'd finally sold a house. That's when it started, my affair with Ivy. When he sent me off with her for the first time and had me stand in for him at an Aerosmith concert. Great seats, too. He'd given her the tickets for her birthday, but didn't make an effort to see the show with her.

Like I said, a world-class idiot.

Ivy and I had some drinks, took a cab back to Dylan's place

where she was staying at the time, and thanks to an unexpected malfunctioning furnace, ended up taking a dip in the hot tub to warm up. In the dead of winter and on an unspoken dare, we stripped naked, tip-toed through the freezing snow, and climbed into that hot tub where we wasted no time fucking like rabbits.

Twice.

It became a near-daily occurrence after that, us hooking up.

I don't know that either of us ever planned for it to happen, it just *did.*

And then it didn't stop.

She kept showing up at my place, or Dylan would ask me to meet up with Ivy at his place for some event he *unfortunately wasn't going to make it home in time* for.

It was never challenging to sneaking around—the man had enabled us entirely—and as much as it pains me to admit, I didn't feel all that bad about it either. Dylan never would have been able to keep up with Ivy long term, and if it hadn't been me, it would've been someone else.

I'd have been a fool not to have swooped in and take her off his hands.

DRIPPING FROM HER CHIN

Sawyer

In the beginning, Ivy and I made a game of our affair. Dylan was so oblivious that there were times we even managed to get it in while he was in the house. See, Ivy had been living with Dylan for a few months by then. I think she gave him some sob story about not being able to renew her lease so, like the nice guy he thought he was, Dylan offered to let her stay with him.

He figured their relationship was moving forward, getting serious, so why not?

But since he was never around, I took it upon myself to take care of his girlfriend—in all aspects of the word. Sneaking around wasn't necessary since he knew she and I hung out, he encouraged it. And the weekly poker night he hosted at his place? Often cancelled at the last minute.

But you know, being the planner that I am, I always arrived earlier than the stated time anyway. *Before* my brother's group text would come through to let the guys know he was stuck at the office, that poker night wasn't happening. I knew Ivy would be there all alone, waiting for me.

I'm a bit of an opportunist, what can I say?

No, man, it's fine. Don't worry about it. Yeah, I'm at your place already. Ivy's here, so we're just going to grab a pizza and catch up on Breaking Bad.

Always so easy.

Always *too* easy.

About a week before we got caught I accidentally told her I loved her. I have no idea what the hell I was thinking—I really wasn't the type to fall in love—but something had come over me. I think I was more in love with the idea of her than I was with her as a person.

But I ran with it, I had no choice once it slipped out.

I wasn't ready to walk away.

Now, if you haven't guessed by now, let me be the first to tell you: Ivy isn't the type of person to take that kind of sentiment lightly. But it was easy for me to say, just three words, followed by some moaning and a deep kiss. She didn't even say it back.

Not with words anyway.

"We shouldn't be doing this," she had teased in between kisses, her eyes deliberately telling me otherwise. I dropped the towel I'd wrapped around my waist after a dip in the hot tub, my dick already standing at attention, ready for her.

"He'll never know." I pulled her closer, kissing her as my hand palmed her ass and squeezed a yelp out of her.

"Oh, but Sawyer, what if he finds out?" She giggled when she said it, the sarcasm dripping from her chin almost like a prelude of what was to come.

It was fun for her, pretending she was worried we'd get caught. She wasn't though, not at all. In fact, I wouldn't be surprised if she *wanted* to all along, given her acquired taste for drama.

"I love you," I'd said.

Yep, that's where it slipped out.

In the heat of a passionate moment, while we poked fun at what we were doing behind my brother's—her *boyfriend's*—back.

The room fell silent despite our heavy breathing.

But it was only a moment later that she dropped to her knees and took me in her mouth right then and there, her tongue swirling in all the places she knew I liked.

And that's how I knew she loved me, too.

She looked so good with her ruby red lips wrapped around my cock, her lipstick smudged along the length of my shaft. She winked and I lost it then, nearly coming down her throat.

But I needed a taste of her, more than anything, I needed to worship her right back. I pulled out of her mouth and helped her up from the floor, only to throw her right back down onto the bed and spread her legs. She squealed, as she often did when she got excited, and I ran my fingers softly down her thighs. Goosebumps prickled beneath them, and she smiled up at me with her signature Fuck Me smirk.

Her body writhed under my tongue as I licked. She bucked and moaned and I continued to taunt her, keeping her close to the edge. When I knew she was ready, I pulled her to me and buried my cock inside her.

That was the last time I ever had sex with my brother's girlfriend.

After that, she wasn't *his* girlfriend anymore.

She was mine.

***

Despite the initial excitement of our affair, I could tell Ivy was bored the moment she moved into my place. We hired help, of course, to get her possessions from point A to point B—from one brother to the next—and she was entertained for a couple months while she turned my house into a *Real Housewives*-esq monstrosity. She spent thousands redecorating every room on the ground floor and half of the upper level, too. But her happiness, her contentment, didn't last. I should have known it wouldn't, but I guess I was surprised.

Still, we christened every room in my house, every countertop, every surface. It didn't matter what time of day or whether we were alone in the house or not—in fact, I recall an entertaining bathroom romp during an investors dinner in our early days.

Still, there was something missing.

And, let's face it, Ivy and I? We've always been perfect on paper. We knew that—it's part of the reason we got married in the first place. And we did everything we could to bring that perfection to everyday life—or at least a semi-believable version of it.

Some days it felt like all the words in our story had been erased, like we'd lost our history and all we had left was the eraser dust scattered within the blank pages.

But then, the whole threesome thing got started, and after that, Ivy went batshit crazy. She became *obsessed* with Alisha.

And that was unheard of.

My wife obsessed over no one, not even me. Things, yes. But, people? Fuck no.

I really should have taken it as a warning sign, an S.O.S., maybe dialed things back a little, let life slow down. Maybe things were just moving too fast. We never got a chance to get comfortable as a couple, let alone a committed partnership. But put yourself in my shoes, okay? When the pussy is right there in front of your face, how do you not reach out for a taste?

I certainly couldn't resist. And the two of them together—*Lila* and Alisha—were like fire and ice, naughty and nice (yes, I went there). I couldn't turn Alisha away no matter how hard I tried, no matter how much I loved my wife.

She'd finally done it; Ivy had found my weakness.

I just didn't expect it to be hers, too.

BODY PARTS

Ivy

People are so easy to manipulate.

It really doesn't take much to convince someone of something they wanted to hear in the first place. A feigned interest, a soft touch of the hand, maybe even an inconspicuous brushing of body parts. It does happen, people use their sexuality to get what they want all the time.

I should know.

That's how I caught Dylan's attention in the first place. See, I knew exactly who he was, I knew of the Thompson family and their wealth. His mother, Bev, had earned a substantial wealth as a Real Estate developer. See, Dylan was a trust fund baby, even before following in his mother's footsteps.

She's a smart woman, that Bev. Wise enough to push a prenup with both of her marriages, yet dumb enough to set so much of her fortune aside for her ungrateful son.

And Dylan? He had a hell of a soft spot for a beautiful woman, especially one who needed him. I knew I had an in, that I could grab his attention.

The fact that he ended up at one of my community theater performances was a lucky accident. I had been working out a way to get some face time with him, he just happened to speed things up for me. The thing is, I didn't think the stepbrother had access to the trust. I *should* have assumed, but Sawyer's own fortune managed to escape my radar initially. I would've started with him had I known.

If you haven't figured me out just yet, you'll notice I excite easily. Sometimes I act before I get all the details get worked out, before I have a plan. That's what happened with Dylan.

How was I to know his trust had a marriage clause?

Five years.

That's how long he would need to be married before his wife would be entitled to any part of his fortune. And I couldn't do it with Dylan, I really couldn't.

That's why Sawyer and I ended up in bed together. That's why I picked *him* instead of Dylan. He was easier to get along with, more attentive and better suited to my sexual desires. Easily manipulated, if you will. A pushover.

A woman has needs, you know, and Sawyer was more than willing—more than *capable*—of meeting mine in Dylan's frequent absence. I would have been a crazy to walk away from such an opportunity.

The thing is, while my initial intentions were to tap into Dylan's bank accounts, I didn't have the patience to wait for the man. He may have been wealthy, but he was dragging his feet on committal—even more so after I moved into his condo—and awfully stringent with his cash.

I didn't have time for stringent.

But finding out Sawyer's pockets were deep, too? That was a good day. He certainly wasn't a trust fund baby like his stepbrother, but *some* of that money was his, thanks to his father's bartering. Plus, he was working in the financial industry by then—he had man-made wealth on top of the trust allocations, and let's be real—that's a hell of a lot better. That's stability.

So yes, the opportunity to seduce him was enthralling, and when it finally presented itself?

Easy peasy.

What I didn't expect was his temper.

Sawyer could be nasty—and he was quick to show that demon, to remind me of its existence. It didn't take long for me to realize that the best way to tamper that anger was to simply appease him, to go along with his plans, feed into his desires, and essentially submit to him.

Fortunately, for me, there were many benefits to this approach.

Sawyer wasn't the only one with desires, and I planned to stop at nothing to remind him of that. Little did I know, he would come up with a prenup of his own.

With the same five-year clause that Dylan's had.

And we've only been married for four fucking years.

NOT QUITE A CALL GIRL

Ivy

Was it a shit show when Dylan finally found out about Sawyer and me?

Yeah, sure.

But it was kinda hot, too. I couldn't help but imagine the three of us together, both brothers worshiping me, bringing me to ecstasy with the flick of a thumb, a tongue here, the tip of a cock there. A girl can dream, right?

Too bad it didn't go down that way.

Dylan was never into that sort of thing—he didn't like the idea of sharing his woman—and even if he did, I don't think he'd have gone for it considering the third wheel was his own stepbrother. There was the whole betrayal aspect of it, too, I suppose.

The poor guy's ego was hurt, rightfully so. And I get it, no man wants to bear the brunt of that embarrassment.

There was yelling.

Some punches thrown. (also hot!)

Name-calling.

You know, the usual caught-in-the-act type stuff. They were proud, filled with testosterone, brothers on the verge of destruction. One had betrayed the other by stealing his girlfriend right from under his nose.

Honestly, are you surprised? This kind of stuff happens all the time. Dylan and Sawyer were two very good-looking men; naturally anyone with an appreciation for the male form would be happy to go home with either of them.

I'm lucky to have had the pleasure of experiencing them both; albeit not at the same time.

Whatever, I'll take the win.

The truth is, I was already looking for a way to end things with Dylan anyway. He simply beat me to it, sped things along, which is fine. I'm not upset it went down the way it did.

It would have been too awkward facing him had things gone smoothly. Holidays with his family would have been a nightmare. The fight between the brothers was reassurance I'd never have to worry about seeing Dylan—possibly not even his parents—ever again. Sawyer soon strayed from the family, and I got a fancy house in Minneapolis complete with a custom mistress's room, top of the line sex swing, and private bath.

Everything worked out as planned.

What neither of the brothers were privy to, however, was the fact that I wasn't as innocent as I seemed. And despite my initial shock when Sawyer mentioned the swinger's club a couple years later, I may have had a *little* experience dabbling in group sex before I met either of them.

To admit this to Dylan would have been a deal breaker long before my affair with Sawyer—he was a little too vanilla if you know what I mean—and I decided it best not to let Sawyer in on that secret either. He really did get more enjoyment out of it later at the swingers club when he thought it was my first time riding the bull in front of an audience.

I was happy to play into his fantasies, to let him think I'd done it for *him*.

What bothered me, though, was that they both assumed I've never worked a day in my life. It's not true, this ridiculous assumption. In fact, I had been working as a Lady Ann escort for two years before meeting Dylan. Acting surely wasn't paying the bills, so I had to do *something.* And unlike Alisha, I had no preconceived notions that I was meant to work in a corporate office, that I wasn't cut out for the sex industry. I knew I was entirely capable of taking my clothes off for money.

So I did.

I was a lot better at concealing my identity than she was, too. Lady Ann's was discreet; the regulars were elite members of society, their bank accounts padded well enough to keep tips in the thousands even on a slow night.

The acting gig? I gave it a go for a bit, tried my hand at smaller productions. But it wasn't long before Mom and Dad decided they were done supporting their oldest daughter, that they were tired of paying my rent and hearing excuses about why I couldn't afford gas for my car.

That's when it started.

I was on my own for the first time, fiercely seeking independence in a way I'd never imagined I would. I left home and never went back.

The party circuit turned out to be quite lucrative. I worked the bachelor parties, private events, stuff like that where the money was easiest because the clientele was mostly just a bunch of married dudes looking to cheat on their wives and pretend they hadn't. Because, you know, it was *just a stripper.*

Fucking idiots.

But, to each their own, right? I didn't care who they were or why they were there, as long as they paid cash and didn't have a choking fetish. The johns had money. Lots of it. And if you were good? If you did just a *little* bit more than hang on their muscle-y arm in a short, sexy dress, they always threw a little extra your way.

And I wasn't afraid to toe the line.

At first it was just hand jobs. A happy ending in a dark corner of the room? *No big deal, happy to help.* And hey, every once in a while one of them would finger me while I jerked them off, so it worked out for me, too. But once I got a taste, I wanted more.

And so did they.

Hand jobs turned into blow jobs, turned into straight-up fucking—it didn't even matter that there were other people in the room. In fact, it was encouraged that everyone join in, especially the ladies.

We earned more that way.

We got invited back that way.

Eventually, the calls kept coming, and I kept showing up. Showered, waxed, and ready for anything, I was a Lady Anne escort. Not quite a call girl, too classy to be a hooker, and nowhere near enough junk in my trunk to strip on a stage for singles.

It was the best paycheck I ever earned.

And I gave it up for a while, just to see if I could. Then I met Dylan, I met Sawyer.

I didn't need the job anymore, not really. I missed it, sure, but for a while things were just fine without it. That is, until Dylan decided his job was more important than me, but even then, I had Sawyer's attention to fall back on. Our affair kept me satisfied, entertained.

Until it didn't.

It wasn't long before Sawyer was off doing the very thing he'd chastised his brother for—working longer hours, attending lavish parties with his business partners to earn his keep. And I was okay with it at first; what he lacked in romanticism he made up for in cash and gifts.

But when Alisha came into our lives, everything changed. It wasn't about me anymore, our attention was on her. On keeping her.

It was when he started seeing Alisha behind my back that triggered things for me, that set things in motion. He'd broken the very code he himself had written to ensure our marriage remained in tact when all was said and done.

So I figured why not? Why not get a little something more out of this myself? I went back to the swinger's club, then to a few underground brothels, and I had some fun of my own. Even opened a new bank account in my name, threw every dime and ass-crack-crinkled dollar I had saved into it, and still continued to collect my monthly stipend from my loving husband. And despite his reservations, Sawyer was gracious with his wallet, let me tell you.

So trust me when I say, I had no problem getting back into the swing of things after Sawyer left. I didn't even wait for the dust to settle. I downed a liter of vodka and worked a bachelor party a couple hours after he walked out the door. Made a good chunk of change that night, I did.

Take it from me, the best cure for a broken heart is sex, even better if you mix in some booze.

My one complaint? Alisha wouldn't come with me; she was wrapped up in Dylan, ready to settle down and give it all up to start a family. She wasn't even returning my phone calls by that point, and that was really the start of the downward spiral that got me here: her selfishness.

Like I said before, I live for revenge.

And in my eyes? I've been betrayed.

TIDE ME OVER

Sawyer

There seems to be some contention around my former relationship with Alisha; I'd like to clear that up if you don't mind. Ivy seems to be under the impression that our marriage failed *because* Alisha left us. It's partially true, sure, but it's not *the* reason. Ivy and I tried to make it work without Alisha for a little while, even reacquainted ourselves with the swingers club for a bit, although I had a feeling there was a little more going on there than she was willing to admit.

And it worked for a while, we got off on it, don't get me wrong. But Ivy was off her game; she wasn't really *in* it because the other person in our bed wasn't Alisha and that was all that mattered to her.

She let it get to her head, if you ask me.

We were tainted—she and I—after Alisha left us. I didn't know how to fix us, didn't have a single fucking clue, and no idea where to start.

So, I did the only thing I could think of—after months of exhausting every other effort, I asked Ivy to try role playing for me. Was it wrong for me to ask her to dress up like Alisha? To *be* her in hopes that it would save our marriage? Sure. I'll give you that.

Look, despite what you might think, I do have a conscience. I offered up the suggestion anyway; nothing else was working and I had nothing more to lose. She could have said no, but she didn't.

She had a choice.

And she made it.

But she played the role terribly, unconvincingly.

The wigs never looked right on her. It was too obvious she wasn't who she was trying to be—I knew what was underneath the facade just as well as she did. Ivy couldn't seem to cover that mole on her neck either. Alisha didn't have a mole.

And let's be real fucking honest here—she didn't taste like her either. The fact that Ivy was an impostor was front and center in my mind, and my dick knew it, too. She lacked her usual confidence.

Some actress she was.

The thing is, nothing compared to the feeling that came over me—came over us—when the three of us were in a room together. We were electric. Intense. Born of another element. Even Ivy would agree there was something special there.

We were lost without Alisha.

Our sex life suffered. *We* suffered. And Ivy got angry. My wife wasn't one to let shit go. She knew what her body wanted.

And she set out to get it.

It was Ivy who decided to try and win her back.

Hell, it's not like we loved each other anymore, and if she tells you otherwise, she's full of shit. The thing is—and my brother would roll over in his grave if he knew this—Ivy and I only got married to piss Dylan off. Sure, we had a vested interest in one another, even liked each other for a while there. And at the time, the sex *was* cutting it. She was a dirty girl hiding behind a thick head of blonde hair. All it took was a little persuasion to get her to come out of her shell.

And I knew she had it in her, I really did.

I just didn't think she'd make such a colossal mistake.

***

In the beginning, finding Alisha was nothing more than a simple twist of fate, a happy accident. I kept her to myself for a bit, but knew I'd eventually introduce her to Ivy, too.

The swingers club was fun, don't get me wrong, but Ivy and I hadn't been formally initiated yet by then and things were moving a little slower than I would have liked. Sometimes I needed a little extra to tide me over. Ivy knew this, I'd been upfront about my sexual desires from the start of our relationship.

It was an honest mistake, finding her, though. I was online, looking for live orgies to watch or one of those XXX websites where you can tell the actors what to do and they'll do it in real-time.

I found *Lisha's Bedroom* instead.

And my God, she was gorgeous.

I mean, Ivy was hot, yes, but Alisha? *Fuck.* Alisha was in a class all her own. I caught her live stream every day for at least two weeks before I told Ivy about her.

That's when the private sessions started. They were expensive, yes, but worth every penny, every minute.

Ivy and I watched her together after that, most often with my dick buried inside of her. She was just as turned on as I was watching Alisha, fantasizing about the three of us together, the ecstasy. Ivy was there with me during those sessions, always watching or stroking me with our eyes glued to Alisha on the laptop screen.

It was Ivy's idea to let Alisha in on our little secret, to invite her over to play with us.

How was I supposed to know she'd actually show up? I didn't think she'd agree to it, but apparently the idea of a threesome was appealing to her too, so she did.

And it was fucking magic.

From the second she walked through the front door I was addicted. She was a drug I was ready and willing to get high on regardless of the ramifications, marriage vows be damned.

Honestly, if you were to ask me if I'd go back and do it again, the answer would be a resounding yes.

It wasn't long before Alisha and I started our little side gig, and that's when I started to see the change in Ivy, the jealousy, the obsession. She knew, but I told myself she didn't.

And while I kind of tricked Alisha into meeting up with me alone that first time—she was under the impression Ivy would be there too—the hotel getaway weekend probably never should have happened. Although, I think if you were to ask Alisha, she'd agree it was worth it. She would've shown up either way.

Was I surprised when she asked why Ivy wasn't there?

No.

The arrangement was clear—we were not to engage in sexual activity unless all three of us were present. We had all agreed, and I understood the rule—hell, I was the one who wrote it.

And Alisha? She was the unbiased party; what did she have to lose by overlooking that one simple rule? She got fucked either way, and that was the only end goal for her.

That weekend was the start of it all really—it also happened to be the first time my brother laid eyes on the woman he'd eventually talk into marrying him.

I didn't see that plot twist coming.

It really was bullshit that he'd take her right from under my nose. But then again, I suppose Ivy and I did the same to him.

Karma really *is* a bitch.

UNINTENTIONALLY VULNERABLE

Ivy

The whiskey goes down smooth despite the trail of fire it leaves on the way down. It numbs me from the inside and I welcome the protective shield it offers, use it to mask the pain.

Life is easier to manage with blinders on, especially the shit no one wants to think about. Like relationships and threesomes gone wrong.

That'll getcha every time.

I've been drinking too much lately, I know this. I would slow down, maybe take it easy with the alcohol, but every time the thought crosses my mind I only want it more.

I like to think this newfound crutch is still temporary, just a necessary distraction from the atrocities of the life I'm currently living, but even that sounds like an excuse.

This too, shall pass.

I tip my head and throw back another shot before paging through the thick document in front of me. Anger bubbles in my belly alongside the whiskey and I catch snippets of the rubbish within the pages.

Dissolution of Marriage.

I didn't think he'd go through with it.

Call me naive, but I really thought we could could fix this, that Sawyer just needed some time to cool off and we'd be fine after a little break, maybe even come out stronger in the end. A little time apart to reflect never hurt anyone, right?

I thought I had nothing to worry about.

We would live separately long enough to come to the realization that we can't live any way other than together. And once we did, we'd be monogamous, no more outside partners, no more threesomes, no more Alishas. Just us.

I was so wrong.

I guess it's true what they say—the sanctity of marriage really *is* lost. After all, a binding contract can be torn to shreds in an instant, so where does its true value really lie? Nothing is set in stone until we die, and by that point the only stone being set is the one used to mark our own grave; completely useless to the dead, a benefit only to the living.

I drain the rest of my drink and set the empty glass on the marble counter with more force than necessary. It breaks and slices through the skin on my palm, the broken shards scattering to the floor. I watch as if in slow motion, as they sparkle against the ambient lighting; they're so small, yet so hazardous.

Unintentionally vulnerable.

Like me.

It hardly seems fair, this divorce. *I* made all the scarifies here, not *him*. And maybe that's why we are where we are now. Maybe I bent him a little *too* far, gave him a little too much freedom.

Maybe Sawyer needed a little more push back every now and then, a wife who fought for him, not against him.

Irreconcilable differences.

Sawyer would say we never really loved each other to begin

with, but I'm not so sure that's true. Maybe for him, but it's not the case for me. I think I was only meant to fill the void until he found someone else, someone better suited for his public image.

But even that doesn't make sense, not really.

Alisha certainly can't service him anymore, not in her current predicament, so I know it's not her he's held up on. And the odds of him finding another woman like me, someone who's willing to marry him *and* let him fuck other women on the side? *Please.*

My hand throbs and tiny droplets of blood land on the counter in splotches. I reach for a napkin and examine the cut; it's not deep, just enough to keep bleeding.

Suddenly exhausted, I stand, leaving the mess on the floor, the napkin wrapped around my hand and the unsigned papers on the counter.

For now, they don't exist.

***

"Good morning, Mrs. Rogers. Sleep well?" Caramie asks when I make my way to the kitchen the next morning. I give her a nod and nothing more; the Susie Homemaker look on her face is enough to make me gag. She plays the part almost *too* well lately, and I can't stand the air of confidence around her-.

No one should be *that* good at life.

"Tea? Just boiled a fresh pot of water," she says reaching for the kettle. "Although, I'm not sure why you haven't switched to one of those Keurig things yet. They're much more efficient for a single party."

"I'm not single," I mutter, the edge in my voice making me

sound like a pack-a-day smoker.

Cara points to the papers on the counter.

Oh yeah, that's right.

I forgot to take them to my office before heading to bed last night. Shame on her for reading them. Though, I suppose I would've too, had I been in her position.

I fight the urge to remind her nothing is official yet, that I haven't signed a damn thing. She knows about my situation, but only in pieces. I don't like the thought of trusting her with anything that important. She still thinks Dylan is Sawyer's son.

Hasn't met him yet either, but I've talked about him plenty, mostly while under the influence and therefore against my will, but it still counts. I don't want her to get the wrong impression of my husband; I still think he'll be coming home eventually.

I grab a mug and hold it out to her as she pours water over the teabag. "Where's the baby?"

"Asleep," she answers semi-smugly, like it were something I should already know. I swear, the kid's schedule changes by the week. How am I supposed to keep up with so much on my mind?

I take a seat at the breakfast counter, not at all surprised to see that Caramie has cleaned up the glass from last night's spill. She catches me staring at the floor.

"All cleaned up," she says, and I swear I hear a glint of pride in her voice. Like I should be proud she did her damn job. There's condescension seeping from her pours this morning and I can't say I care for it. I'm not sure I want to know why, but I ask anyway.

"What's with you today?"

"I'm sorry?"

"You're in a mood. What's up?"

"Nothing at all, Mrs. Rogers. Just a beautiful day."

It's Ivy, thanks.

"Right."

We sit in silence for a few minutes, the tension festering for reasons that remain unknown. "Your son is sleeping well lately," she says, not that I needed the update.

I don't say anything, just nod.

"Will you have a few minutes to visit with him when he wakes up?"

"When will that be?"

"Around eight."

"I'll be gone by then. Appointments today," I say, suddenly realizing the excuse means I'll need to leave the house today. Caramie nods with a judgment riddled expression, it's subtle but I know I saw it. I equally want to slap her and kiss her, but I don't care for her tone this morning, so I do neither.

"I'll take this upstairs," I say, gently tipping the steaming mug in her direction. She smiles, and pours some for herself, a look of contention on her face as she brings the mug to her lips and takes a sip.

I'm not sure what to make of it, her new attitude, but at this point, I'm far too hungover to worry about it.

DICK IN MY HAND

Sawyer

I didn't want to send the papers.

I knew Ivy wouldn't react well to them, but what am I supposed to do? Sit here with my dick in my hand while she raises my dead brother's son on *my* dime? No, this divorce is necessary. I've worked too hard to get where I'm at, to build my clientele and make a name for myself. It's time to cut her off. Ivy doesn't deserve my money, not after the shit she's pulled.

I'm done supporting her.

And hiring a nanny to take care of her love-child, no less? I'm not about to support another man's kid, okay? I didn't knock her up, why should I have to suffer the consequences?

Kids were never in the cards—never even on the table—for us. Ivy knew that, she still *knows* that. We discussed it ad nauseam—*she* even agreed she wanted nothing to do with dirty diapers and snot-nosed kids. So whose fault is this divorce, really?

Ivy remains convinced our demise has everything to do with Alisha, with my stepbrother. But she's wrong. This divorce is the result of her trying to trap me with that damn baby.

And she tried, believe me.

She thought she had me, too, that she could play it off like I was the one who knocked her up all along. Little did she know.

I hate kids.

That's why I had a vasectomy when I was twenty-five, a birthday gift to myself, *thank you very much*. And no, I didn't bother to share that little fact with my wife. Why would I when kids weren't part of the plan? I kept her in the dark on the subject until *after* she told me "we" were expecting.

The fact that she went out of her way to feign happiness, to tell me how excited she was when she made the announcement wasn't lost on me either. She thought she'd finally secured her cut of my wealth, that there was no way I'd deny "our" child the life of luxury they deserved.

And I'm not gonna lie, the look on her face when I not only announced my inability to conceive a child, but produced documentation to prove it, was priceless.

Talk about an elephant in the room.

When the truth finally came out, when she told me what she'd done, that she'd fucked Dylan and the kid was the seed of my stepbrother, that's when I knew for sure.

She had killed him.

I knew what it meant, why she did it, and can't say it surprised me. She was determined to take it to her grave, too.

She wanted Alisha back.

Having Dylan's baby was her royal flush.

But she'd shown her cards too early and look where that got us, where it got Alisha.

And the thing is, I doubt Ivy even considered our prenup while she took advantage of my brother. It's void now, invalid, washed away like a turd on the sidewalk. She'd had an affair and was pregnant with another man's child. She wouldn't stand a chance at alimony under those circumstances. I would've been an idiot not to get the hell away from this shit show before the crowd started booing.

This is for the best.

For both of us.

***

On Tuesday I head to the office early, my stress level rising with the knowledge that Ivy has been served with the divorce papers. I know she won't go down easy, I get that. I can't say I blame her; we had a good thing going there for a while. It'll be tough to let go of that, but she's given me no choice.

The kid is a deal-breaker.

My assistant, Krissy, hasn't arrived yet, so I drop a muffin at her desk—banana nut, her favorite—for later, knowing full-well she'll return the favor down the road. It's what we do, what *normal* people do for their co-workers.

It's important for me to appear normal, to maintain my blue-collar image if I intend to remain in this industry. My side gig depends on it.

But it's a struggle some days, today especially.

By ten a.m. I'm more anxious than I was on the way in. I'm pacing my office, wearing a path in the carpet while I try to make sense of everything that's happened over the last year. My thoughts won't settle, and for some reason, all I can think about is making love to my wife. Making love to Alisha.

The images play like a movie in my mind, and oh, how I wish I could see them in the flesh. That they were real, tangible, and happening right here and how.

Visions of Ivy as she licks Alisha's pussy.

I miss that, the three of us together.

I think I always will.

And now I'm trying to scare away a boner like a teenage boy. Apparently, my dick is making all the decisions today. I mumble a curse word and shove my laptop and some documents into my briefcase. I can't concentrate, there's no point in being here.

"Heading out for the day, sir?" Krissy asks when I step out, the muffin I left her now a mere pile of crumbs left behind on a napkin.

It feels like a metaphor.

"Yes, my apologies. I'm fighting a migraine today. Clear my calendar, will you?"

"Yes, sir. See you tomorrow." I wave and close my office door behind me.

"Thanks for the muffin!"

***

Twenty minutes later I'm home, stripped naked, and ready to rub one out on the couch. I grab my laptop and pull up the video, the one I saved for occasions such as this.

I'm not supposed to have this footage, but I do, and I watch it often: the night my wife and I were initiated into the swingers club. They said no phones, no cameras, it was a well-communicated rule, but there was no way I was going to miss out on the opportunity to look back at this.

It's all about who you know and how much cash you can slide under the table.

I tap the play button on the video and lean into the couch, the leather cool beneath my ass.

"Do you want me to fuck your wife?"

I look over at Ivy and the way she's rubbing herself and sucking her bottom lip is almost enough to make me cum right here and now. She wants it, she wants that dick, and she wants me to tell her it's okay to have it.

I nod, and he summons her with a finger pointing toward the ground, motioning for her to drop to her knees, to pleasure him. And she does, she takes his cock like a champ. I sit back in the armchair, pumping my own fist slowly, watching in awe while my wife deep-throats another man's cock.

She looks so fucking beautiful.

I had no idea she'd look so good with someone else's dick in her mouth.

Watching my wife with another man was a high like I'd never experienced. And I've been high plenty of times, so I'm not just saying that. It was the pleading look in her eyes as she took that dick that really did it for me. The way they rolled back in her head every time he pounded into her.

She liked it rough, she did.

And she was grateful when I admitted I paid to have the session recorded. We watched it together often in the beginning, before Alisha came into our lives. We even tried bringing it back once after she was gone, when we struggled to find each other again, but Ivy said it wasn't as much of a turn on as it once was.

That was upsetting.

It still turns me on just the same.

I guess nobody ever tells you that once you get involved in group sex, one-on-one will never be the same, never as satisfying. That's what made that night so monumental; it was the start of everything that broke us.

Why I continue to torture myself by re-watching it, I'll never know.

But it makes me come every time, and right now it's the desperate release that I need.

LASH OUT

Ivy

I don't expect it, the day she calls.

It's late afternoon, and I should be getting ready for a night out, but I can't seem to get motivated enough to climb out of bed. Something has felt off all day, almost like a premonition of sorts, like I knew something big was about to happen.

My heart pounds in my chest, the anticipation nearly unbearable as my cell vibrates in my hand. If I stare at it too long she'll be gone, so this is it. *The* moment I've been waiting for.

"This is a prepaid call from an inmate at the Smithson Women's Penitentiary..."

"Hello?"

The line is quiet, but she's there, breathing softly into her end of the phone. I'm sure it must be hard for her, making this call, so I wait patiently for her to speak. I don't want to rush her, not after all this time.

"I got your letter," she says finally.

Not the first words I expected, but they're words and they've come from her mouth, so I take them greedily. She sounds different, harder somehow. More reserved, closed off. I've been sending her letters for months now, sometimes two a week, and she's never once written back, let alone picked up the phone and called. I knew she needed time. I've respected her boundaries, it's the least I could do.

I knew she'd come around.

"Which one?" I ask, although I hope she's been reading them all, admiring the pictures I've shared with her, the words I've written on the pages.

"All of them."

I nod as though she can see me, emit a sharp intake of breath and I'm trying to reign it in, not to get upset, but my broken heart is fragile, and it wants to lash out. I need explanations, nurturing. Something to show me that what we had wasn't nothing.

That I did what I did for a reason.

"So, why now then?" I ask, an accidental edge to my voice. My intention to be nice, to be patient with her, already resolved. "It's been a year—an entire *year*—and you're just now calling me?"

"I didn't know what to say," she admits, her tone soft, but unapologetic. This is the start of *her* revenge, her chance to wrong me right back. In a way, I suppose I owe her this; I deserved her silence, and now her harsh words.

"And do you now? Know what to say, I mean."

"Why'd you do it?"

"Ah, come on...I think you can do better than that."

"Why did you do it?" she repeats, this time the words hold weight, they're an arsenal of pain and she tosses them in my direction with purpose.

"Lisha— "

"I have a right to know!"

"Last I checked, you no longer have rights to a damn thing,"

I snap. "You're in *prison*."

"Yeah? And whose fault is that? You can't expect me to just move on, Lil—*Ivy*." She pauses, and I picture her leaning against the wall, her forehead nestled against cold brick, a tear rolling down her cheek. "My husband is dead because of you."

She says the words now, possibly out loud for the first time. I bet it feels good to say them, to know I've heard them and maybe even been hurt by them.

But I've expected this.

I've waited for this call, to feel her anger, her resentment.

To understand her pain.

I miss her, but I don't tell her this, I can't. She's not ready to hear it. She just needs more time.

Silence is truly the only way, as hard as it is to give it to her. I sigh and say the only other words I can think to say. "You made your bed, Lisha. What happens next is up to you."

"Wai—"

I end the call, my body shaking as I stare at the silent phone in my hand. I didn't mean to hang up on her, but what was I supposed to do? I know they record these calls, and I'm not about to say something stupid, get myself in trouble. She baited me. She *wanted* me to say something incriminating.

I'd thought we were past that.

But this phone call changes things, and I'm sure she knows it, too. We're speaking again, and that's the first step to getting her back, to finding *us* again.

I'm still so angry, but this fight, this feud of ours is in our blood, coursing through our veins like a virus that can never be cured. This history between us is terminal unless we overcome it together, and soon she'll realize it too. She *has* to.

Alisha loves me.

She *will* come back to me.

SCHMOOZE, YOU LOSE

Sawyer

There's a lot of schmoozing in the finance industry.

I should know, I'm a finance guy.

To be honest, sometimes I hate it, but the money is good and we all know that's what makes the world go 'round. What they tell you in business school, and that I've found entirely accurate by the way, is that people want to invest their money with guys they trust. They want a solid character, someone who has more than a little stake in the game, something to lose: a family man.

I'm not a family man, not by any means, but I'm good at pretending to be.

My job depends on it, so I do it. That means Ivy did, too. Now, if you haven't figured it out by now, my wife doesn't like to be told what to do, let alone abide by societal norms. She can be a challenge, but she listens when she has to, when I tell her it's time to put on a show.

She likes money.

She'll do anything for it.

Our arrangement worked for us; for a while anyway, living a privileged life in the public eye, so to speak. I mean, we're not celebrities, not by anyone's standards, but we've become pillars of the community. I'm the guy that invests in the small local business. The guy who throws money into charitable causes whether he believes in them or not, goes to church on Sundays despite his many sins. There are eyes on us even when they're not looking. It's the nature of the game, so we do it.

Ivy, being a former "actress", knew how to turn it on when necessary. She even helped me land one of my biggest accounts, not to say I agreed with her methods, but she secured a once in a lifetime deal for me. I think that's why she feels entitled to my money now that things are less than kosher between us.

It was innocent at first, our approach at the investor's luncheon. A garden party at the home of our firm's president, Alexander Bookman. Unbeknown to him, I had insider information on the client and that's why I fought so hard to be put on the account. Luckily, my boss, great guy that he is, went out on a limb by letting me take the lead.

As we waited for our guests to arrive, I stood locked in conversation with Bookman, a frosted glass of beer in my hand. My fourth of the day, although I'd drunk the first three before the catering crew had arrived, so to everyone else it was my first and I was nursing the shit out of it. Secret of the trade for you there.

Bookman had been yammering on for a good twenty minutes about some new investment opportunity with an up and coming sports agency in Minneapolis, and I had grown bored just a few minutes into his spiel. It wasn't that I was uninterested, just that I'd heard the same monologue from him a week earlier.

And he wasn't the target I was after, anyway. He knew my mind was elsewhere, and didn't take offense when I politely excused myself to meet with the head of EHC.

The Ehrens-Havenbrook Corporation was expected to make

a killing for anyone involved, and more so for me if I played my cards right.

I wanted in.

I'd studied the business model for ten days straight, and from what I could tell, on paper they had a justified business—with plenty of means to launder a shit ton of drug money on the side. Now, I'm not going to assume you're one to approve of such a thing, but here's a little newsflash for you: I'm not against money laundering. I'll take my cut and never lose a wink of sleep.

The business cover was good, the paperwork and financial accounts solid, untraceable.

That's why Ivy was across the yard flirting with the only guy there who mattered, *the* reason we made an appearance at the dog and pony show.

Connor Ehrens.

The man who was going to make me rich.

I had heard Ehrens had a thing for petite blondes, liked the way they flirted with him, and that was a category my wife fell into easily. The rest of her body worked in our favor, too.

I told her the plan over breakfast that morning; she was on board. "Whatever you need," she'd said. What I needed was to land that fucking client.

I watched Ivy place a hand on Ehrens's chest. She giggled at something he said that I doubt she found remotely funny, and batted her long eyelashes at him. His face softened, but I imagine other parts of him hardened right up.

I hadn't meant to watch it go down, the suspense was nauseating, but I found myself hiding behind a well-manicured hedge like a peeper while she worked him over.

She flirted.

She flattered.

Eventually she took him upstairs to the guest bathroom and that's where I lost sight of the target. I suppose it was to be expected, given the circumstances, so I wasn't upset. I'd seen my wife with other men plenty of times by then. My biggest complaint was that I didn't get to watch.

It was later though, after the party, when I realized the small kink in our plan.

Sending Ivy in to hook the shark was a mistake, a rookie move on my part. We played our hand awfully early and I should have known they'd take advantage of her involvement after that, that they'd want to keep her.

I should have seen it coming.

She did give one hell of a blow job.

We landed the client.

But only if Ivy was willing to work for Ehrens, too.

***

"You may have outdone yourself with Ehrens today," I told her later that evening. I undid my tie and slid it off my neck, fingering the material and watching Ivy remove her heels, my eyes locked in on her toned legs.

"I did what you asked me to do."

"And then some," I muttered with a smirk.

"Don't do that," she snapped, pointing a finger in my direction. "Don't patronize me. *You* sent me in there."

I managed a laugh and took her hand, positioning it over the growing bulge in my pants. She gasped and massaged me through the material before shoving me down onto the bed.

I welcomed her need to regain control, to put me in my place.

She took the tie from my hand and wrapped it around my wrists, knotting it tightly through the beams of our headboard. My dick throbbed as her hands found my belt and went to work.

My wife knew she had the upperhand.

She had earned her reward.

And it was going to cost me.

ATTENTION-SEEKING

Sawyer

Ivy never did manage to fit in with the other wives.

And she knew it, of course she did. I think it's safe to say her awareness of the issue caused more damage than good. She tried too hard, always going the extra mile, but being overly fake about it. They saw right through her act, and I can't say I blame them.

Sometimes I think she did it on purpose, but there's no sense in arguing a point I can't prove.

One of the wives in particular, Bethany, seemed to have it out for her. Naturally, she and Ivy despised each other, and boy did they make sure the rest of us knew about it.

I don't know what it is about men in finance, but we tend to marry the attention-seeking-housewife types, those beautiful women seemingly placed on God's green earth for their beauty and little else. Don't scoff at that, you know it's true, that they're out there.

Ivy certainly dressed the part, she did her best to keep up with status quo, but eventually Bethany managed to tear her down. Right down to the stump.

And you can't fault her for it either, it happens with the weak ones sometimes. When they're not careful, those loose canons have been known to sink ships.

Ivy was never careful.

She was reckless, abandoned when she should have kept her shit together. It was bad before it was ever good I guess.

The attention from Alisha's trial didn't help either, why would it? These women wanted the inside scoop, they wanted Ivy to spill the beans about her involvement, but all that did was set her up for further ridicule. The gossip started and ended with my wife, but what she didn't realize—what she *couldn't* possibly have known—is that she was slowly digging her own grave.

All she had left to do was jump in.

Lie down flat.

They'd shovel the dirt in right on top of her the first chance they got.

I tried to fix it, I did. Little chats with the wives here and there at cocktail parties and dinner nights, a comment to one of the partners—the husbands who did their best to rein in their wives. I'd hoped it'd clear the air, show everyone Ivy wasn't the conniving temptress she came across as.

You and I both know she is.

So did they.

My attempts had a tendency to make things worse for her in the long run. My kind words and stories about her good deeds within the community—how she organized the church bake sale, sat co-chair for the annual fundraiser—they all seemed to have the opposite effect.

Ivy does whatever her husband tells her to.

That's the only way she gets to collect her allowance, you know.

Damn, those women were ruthless.

I can't say I blame them; Ivy's drama is nothing if not entertaining.

"Sawyer?"

I'm in the grocery store, grabbing stuff for dinner when I see her.

Bethany.

She's looking pristine as always, even for the grocery store, as she tucks a strand of hair behind her ear with a freshly-manicured finger. *Just the woman I didn't care to see today.*

"Bethany, good to see you," I say, careful of my tone.

"I thought that was you...didn't realize you do your own shopping these days. How have you been?" she tips her head in faux empathy, her hand embracing my forearm.

"Hanging in," I say, aware that while I don't want it, I need her sympathy. I have an image to uphold here, and my soon-to-be-ex-wife isn't making things any easier for me, despite our time apart.

"I heard about Ivy," she continues before I get another word in. I nod, but don't bite. I know whatever I say will make it around the block when she starts running her mouth the second she walks out of here.

"I'm in a bit of a hurry."

"Oh, sure. My apologies. Don't let me keep you." She pats my arm, her fingers lingering longer they should. "Before you go?"

"Hm?"

"The girls and I would like to put together a care package for Ivy and the baby. You know, since she wasn't so keen on the shower idea. Anything in particular you guys need?"

And there it is.

The question I'd hoped to avoid.

Our social circle is still under the impression I fathered Ivy's son.

It's time to let the cat out of the bag, give these women a new reason to talk behind my wife's back. This time she deserves it.

"He's not my son," I say.

And then I abandon my cart in the store and make a beeline for the door.

I don't need this shit today.

KATY FUCKING PERRY

Ivy

I type out a text to Sawyer and press send before I can talk myself out of it. I know I shouldn't be contacting him, but I can't help myself. I want to hear from him, see him. He rarely responds, but I know he loves the dirty messages I send him, the naked pictures. He's a stubborn mule, but a sucker for a wet pussy and I have no problem reminding him how wet mine can get for him.

The hope is that he can't resist, that he'll show up at the front door, all his belongings in tow, and come crawling back to me.

That he'll forgive me.

Sometimes a man just needs to be reminded of what they have, what they're about to lose if they follow through with their dumb decisions.

Sawyer is one of those guys.

I still don't think he'll follow through with the divorce. I haven't signed the papers and it'll be months before a judge will force me to. Even then, it won't be the end of us.

There is no end to us.

I set the phone on the counter and nurse a glass of Moscato. The day has gotten away from me. A lot of days seem to be getting away from me lately. But it's fine.

I don't have a problem.

It's not like anyone is around to notice most of the time, tonight especially. Caramie left hours ago for a night out with her friends. She doesn't have much of a social life, which bodes well for me given our current arrangement, but I'd be lying if I said I don't miss her tonight. I feel her absence. Good thing baby Dylan is such a good sleeper; not a peep all night.

I like to think I'm okay being here alone, but when I hear her come in through the garage entrance, my pulse picks up a smidge. I sit up straighter on the bar stool and try to look less drunk, a little less depressed, as I plaster on a smile.

"Ivy? Are you in here?" Caramie's voice calls around the hall corner. She steps into view and manages to take my breath away. She's gorgeous in a tight little black dress, her blue suede pumps elongating her toned legs.

All the wine goes to my head as I stand.

I can't help myself.

I walk to her, my breath heavy when I reach out and touch her hair. I see the confusion on her face, but she's intrigued, I know she is. I see that, too, feel it in my bones. She doesn't push me away as I move closer, and I wonder if maybe she's been expecting this all along, if she feels the attraction, too.

I intend to use words, but none come out.

Instead it's her hand I feel on my hip, drawing me closer as if letting me know this is okay. That she wants me, too. Her lips meet mine, and, *oh—they're so fucking soft.* She tastes like strawberries and mint and wine coolers and I want more.

I whimper, and she does, too.

Our bodies relax into one another, a crash of heat between us.

But she pulls away after just a moment, and brings a hand to her mouth, her eyes left searching my own.

"Cara..." I whisper. She takes a step back and her nipples poke through the fabric of her dress, like proof that she liked the way it felt, our kiss, our bodies together. She wants more, but I'm not sure she'll allow herself to take it.

"I'm sorry, Ivy, I..." She stomps off down the hall, the click of her heels echoing on the hardwoods beneath her. I watch her leave, soft brown curls bouncing against her back as she does.

And it's clear then, what just happened. What's about to happen when I eventually follow her down the hall and sneak into her bedroom. She'll give in because that's what women do, what we need to feel human.

Except that when I go to her, she doesn't give in at all. She doesn't let me have her the way I want to, the way I need. Because she's not like me.

I've been a fool to think she'd want me.

But it's not the first time I've been wrong.

***

I slept like shit.

Rejection tends to do that to me.

You'd think I'd be used to it by now, but the sting is fresh, another wound in my weakening armor. My eyes are puffy, but I'm not sure if it's from crying or the bottle of wine I consumed by myself; my guess is both, but if Caramie's downstairs when I grab my morning tea I'll need to go with the wine excuse.

She's used to that one by now.

And she's there, as I knew she would be, sitting at the table nursing a cup of coffee while Dylan sleeps in the playpen beside her. The tension is as palpable as ever, but I drop a tea bag into a mug and pour hot water from the kettle over it before joining her at the table.

"Listen, about last night—" I start, but Caramie silences me with a hand in the air, her face softening like she knows just how much last night hurt me but isn't sure what to do about it.

"Don't even mention it," she says. "It was my fault, really, I shouldn't have—"

"No, don't do that to yourself. I was the one who initiated it, and I'm sorry, but it was nothing. I was just drunk and horny."

I'm not sure if she sees through my feigned nonchalance or not, but I give it a try anyway. The last thing I want is for things to be awkward between us. I need her here, with me, with Dylan.

"It's just that...I would understand if you want to fire me. I shouldn't have—"

"Oh, Cara, no. It was just a stupid kiss. A *kiss.* It was nothing, trust me."

"You sure?"

"Positive. And really, it's *my* fault. I should be the one apologizing. I shouldn't have taken advantage of you like that."

"You didn't take advantage..."

"No?"

She shakes her head, her cheeks suddenly coloring with blush. "It was kinda nice," she says. "I've never kissed a woman before."

"Oh, honey...you really don't know what you're missing, do you?" I tease with a wink.

We sit in silence for a moment, and it's not awkward. Just quiet, a peace offering of sorts. Until a moment later when her laughter fills the room, and she's giggling uncontrollably, her eyes crinkling in that cute way they do when she's amused. "I can't..."

"What is it?"

"It's that...stupid Katy Perry song..." she says between breaths. She clutches her stomach, the laughter apparently giving her an ab workout. The look on her face is priceless as she finishes the thought. "...I can't get that fucking song out of my head!"

Cara had kissed a girl...and she liked it.

LADY ANN

Ivy

I said I wouldn't do it.

That I didn't *need* it.

Apparently, I was wrong, so here I am.

I've returned to Lady Ann's. I know, I know, it's stupid, and I know what you're thinking. I need to move on from my past, start fresh, maybe in a new town, a new home. The problem is, I'm not ready to let go of my old life, of the thrills, the excitement.

The pleasure.

This is the hit I crave.

Things will be different this time around, though. Unlike before, I'm not a paying member of the club. This time it's a career. A business opportunity. Lady Ann herself is paying *me* to be there, on top of the fees and tips I'll make off the customers. I like to think of my newfound employment as an investment opportunity in myself.

I'm not too naive to realize the irony in that statement, but I'll take it considering. Against my will, it seems I'll soon be past my sexual prime, so why not? How long can I keep this up, and at what point will I start *looking* like the cougar I think I am?

My clock is ticking.

Thank God the money is good.

Who knew there was a lucrative side to this business? That it wasn't all orgasms and living out sexual fantasies? Turns out, once you've been in for a while, once Lady Ann trusts you and sees you're good for business, she'll want to use you. She sees your value, the one good card you bring to the table.

So, I work for her now. I'm officially back in the escort business.

And I'm loving it.

I'm still thinking about my shared kiss with Caramie when I head out to Lady Ann's two nights later. There's something about my son's nanny that's been keeping me awake at night. I can't put my finger on it.

Literally.

She's so different from Alisha, from all the other women I've been with. There's an innocence about her. I think I want to take that away from her.

I'm a good fifteen minutes early for work, so I park and kill the engine before unbuckling and grabbing my phone from my purse. I tap the icon for Instagram and head to Caramie's page. We follow each other, more or less so I can ensure she holds up her end of the bargain, which is not to post pictures of my son on social media. My page exists merely to keep tabs on other people, Cara being one of them.

She's kept her word, I don't see any photos with Dylan, nothing suspicious at all really. I run my finger along the screen, scrolling leisurely as I take in the selfies and food-related content. She's not one to post often, but when she does it usually falls into one of those two categories.

I don't understand the purpose, but that must be me showing my age again. Closing the app, I drop my phone back into my clutch and check my makeup in the visor before heading inside.

I'm not inside for long before Lady Ann hands me a slip of paper with an address on it. It takes me by surprise; I'm always assigned to house duty. I'm still new here.

"You and Pen have a pick up tonight," she says. I don't ask questions, that's not what we do around here, but this is a new development; she's never sent me on a house call before. Not that I question her judgment, Lady Ann knows our interests better than anyone; which clients we'll go for and which we won't. She even knows how far we'll go sexually. That's part of her job and why she's so good at it.

But she's never assigned me—or Penelope, for that matter—to a pickup.

It's no surprise that we run drugs through the house, hell, I've helped Sawyer launder money through this place. I just didn't think I'd find myself fetching the goods for her. I can't say I'm against a little bump every once in a while, though, especially considering how well my life is going lately. It is what it is I guess.

Our driver delivers Penelope and me to the location, well aware that showing up alone for a drug pick up with a vagina under your dress is strongly frowned upon. We all know this. It's Whoring 101, right there on the top of the syllabus.

Not that our armed driver will be following us through the door. We're on our own once we get in there.

"Are you nervous?" Pen asks, flipping her long dark hair over her shoulders. It cascades down her back in waves, the curls loose and bouncy. I imagine a john with his fingers wrapped in it, tugging just enough to excite her.

"Earth to Ivy..." she says, snapping her fingers.

"Hm? Sorry, I was thinking about something."

"What's with you?"

"I'm not sure. What did you ask me?"

"I asked if you're nervous."

"Oh. No, why? Should I be?"

"It's our first pick up together. I've never done one before. Have you?" I shake my head, although I didn't necessarily want her to know it was my first job. Why Lady Ann would send two virgins out on a supply pick up was beyond me. But I suppose that's why I'm not the one in charge. I just do what I'm told; the payouts are bigger that way.

But this house looks familiar, like I've seen it before. "Where are we?" I ask the driver; he just shrugs. He's not supposed to speak to us, but it was worth a shot.

"I hear this guy hand-picks his girls," Penelope whispers beside me.

"Is that so?"

"Mmhm, and he's *insanely* wealthy. Older guy, probably forties or so. Doesn't take shit from anyone," she says as we climb out of the car. "And he *always* hand picks his girls. I'm happy we're the chosen ones, he's quite the tipper."

I'm hung up on the fact the she considers *in his forties* older as we climb the front steps and pause at the top. "Ready?" she asks, raising her hand to knock on the expansive wooden door. It opens with a creek and I recognize him right away.

Connor Ehrens.

No wonder I was assigned to pick up tonight.

"What have we here?" Ehrens asks, winking at me.

"Lady Ann sent us for pick up," Penelope says.

"Did she now?"

She nods and sucks her bottom lip into her mouth. She looks like the armature that she is, but I refuse to be the one to tell her. Ehrens doesn't seem to mind, though, he seems to appreciate her innocence. He brings a hand to her chin, his fingers snaking along her neck. "What's your name, gorgeous?"

"Penelope," she says stupidly. She was supposed to give a fake name.

You never forget the fake name.

"Pretty. First time?"

"Yes." She nods.

So much for Plan A.

"Then we may need to show you ladies how things work around here, hmm?" He taunts her, walking slowing around her like she's his prey. I spot another man at the staircase, a handgun attached to his hip, and quickly recognize him as Michael Havenbrook.

I wonder if he knows I can see his erection through his pants.

Dibs, I think.

We step further inside the house and the door closes behind us, a guard standing against it with his arms crossed.

"Lady Ann filled us in," I inform him, sticking to my it's-not-my-first-rodeo charade, despite the fact that these guys likely know otherwise. His eyes dart to mine, his fingers still making their way down Penelope's neck. She drapes an arm around his shoulders, the other resting on his chest.

"Glad to hear it," he says. "Show me what you have for me, Lila."

The mention of my stage name is unexpected; he knows who I am. He could have blown my cover if he wanted to. I take the bait and play along.

"Product first," I say with a teasing tone. "We know how this works."

Ehrens pulls a small bag from his pocket and passes it to me, a conniving smile playing on his lips. "As you wish." He pulls out a second pouch, opening the small baggie, and pops one of the pills onto my tongue. I consider spitting it out, maybe hoarding it under my tongue, but I don't mind the idea of forgetting tonight and decide to swallow it down instead.

"Good girl," he says.

As if on command, I drop to my knees and take his cock in my mouth, Penelope kneeling down beside me. She reaches over and pulls the top of my dress down, exposing my breasts, and my nipples immediately perk up. The sexy stranger at the staircase *(Havenbrook, duh)* joins us, freeing his cock from his pants as he comes up on the other side of me. I take him in my mouth while Pen works on Ehrens; he doesn't take long to finish.

The stranger comes quickly, too, and I'm unexpectedly grateful because the E is starting to kick in and I think I need to lie down.

"Here," Ehrens says, tossing me another bag before shoving his dick back in his pants.

"What's this?"

"A little extra for you. Since you were both so generous with your payment tonight." He winks and opens the door as I stand and struggle to put my tits back into my dress. "I'll see you in a couple days?"

I nod, even though I have no idea whether or not I'll ever be back here. That's not my call to make.

It's amazing what a couple good blow jobs can buy though.

We walk with swagger back to the town car, Penelope giggling as she says, "I don't think we were supposed to suck them off."

She snakes an arm through mine and I laugh with her.

"No, I don't think so either." I'm not opposed to cutting corners, never have been. My moral compass rests easy as always.

"Should we keep the extra E it for ourselves?"

"No, we can't. It could be a test," I say, and she pouts, seemingly bummed to miss out on the high.

But I don't feel an ounce of guilt when I pocket the extra pills for later.

BETWEEN MY LEGS

Ivy

I didn't want to dress too casually. Didn't want to overdress either, if I'm being honest. I think the outfit I chose is rather modest, especially in comparison. Simple skinny jeans and a white blouse. Flats, minimal silver jewelry. My blonde hair now cut to my shoulders, styled in a bouncy bob.

I feel good; pretty even, but not *too* pretty.

She has refused to see me since the day she was convicted, so my efforts will likely be for nothing, slight of a few empathetic glances in my direction from strangers I'll never see again.

I don't know why I keep subjecting myself to this, but I do. I'm here, waiting for her, hoping today will be the day she changes her mind.

"Can you check again, please?" I ask the intake officer. The partition window is covered in finger print smudges, and I can't help but want to clean it. Surely, this place can afford a cleaning service, right? At least to hide the fact that things aren't what they seem once you get through the heavy doors.

The admin removes her hands from the keyboard, a sympathetic tilt of her head tells me she's less sympathetic than she is annoyed. This isn't the first time I've shown up here uninvited for visitor's day. She's turned me down before.

"Mrs. Rogers, you're not on her call list. You're not on her visitor's list. I'm sure she'll let you know if that changes." She pauses, waits for me to step out of line and walk off with my tail between my legs. I don't move, just stand there processing, trying to understand why she won't see me. "Next!" she calls, waving a hand in the air.

"Ma'am? Let's go, come on." A corrections officer takes my elbow and pulls me aside, out of the way so they can assist the next person, someone with an inmate waiting to see them.

My chest hurts.

It shouldn't, not after going through this so many times, but it hurts nonetheless.

Why won't she let me see her?

***

I drive home in a perpetual state of confusion.

I can't be the only one hurting here. Has she even considered what this will do to our son once he's old enough to understand her rejection? He deserves to meet his other mother, he does.

"Fuck!" I scream, the vibrato of my voice rattling my throat. I slam my hands against the steering wheel, the car veering into the other lane, but it's okay because there's no one there. I'm the only car on this deserted road, the only idiot that was sent away before visiting hours are over.

All I want to do is breathe the same air as her, to look at her in the flesh, and tell her I'll find a way to get us out of this.

I just want to get us out of this.

BORROWED TIME

Ivy

Sawyer stops by unannounced around the lunch hour, looking dapper in a three-piece suit as if it isn't a Friday afternoon in the middle of a Midwestern summer. He doesn't even break a sweat. Meanwhile, I'm sunbathing in the backyard—sweat pooling in all major crevices—when I hear the alert from the Ring camera. Caramie's entertaining baby Dylan under the shade of an umbrella, her modest one-piece suit working wonders for her curves.

"I'll get it," I say uncharacteristically. She gives me a look, but I shoo her off. "I need to grab some water anyway."

She nods and I step inside, padding barefoot through the house as I wrap a shawl around my torso. When I open the door to him I can't help but feel under-dressed, grateful at least, that my tits look good in this bikini top. I can't say I'm ready to see him, but he's here and I need to decide what to do with that. There's a pang in my chest as I drink in the sight of him.

"You shouldn't be here," I say, the conviction hidden somewhere far beneath the words when they make their way out of my mouth. It's always been hard to say no to him, to turn him away, but I have to or he will bury me.

"I just need to grab a few things, Ivy," he argues, his eyes lingering on my chest.

"No." I shake my head, no longer trusting my voice.

"This is still my house."

"Not for long," I snap as if those words hold any weight. I know they don't, nothing I say does anymore, but Sawyer doesn't know that yet so I keep pushing. I have to make his life without me as miserable as possible so he'll come home to me.

And yes, that means I'm hoarding his shit.

"Ivy, have you been drinking?"

"What? No, of course not," I lie, wishing I'd had a chance to pop a piece of gum into my mouth. But Sawyer thinks chewing gum is classless, so I rarely have it around.

"I can smell the booze on your breath," he says, leaning closer as I back away. "Just let me in."

I stand there silently, watching Caramie through the window out of the corner of my eye. She scoops up the baby and heads toward the house. He's gumming the noise-making toy he's been playing with (that's better suited for the bottom of the garbage bin), his arms flapping and a smile turning up on his face, the drool dripping down his chin.

He's teething.

Which means he's not sleeping well.

I imagine that leaves Cara pretty tired these days, considering she's the one getting up with him at all hours of the night, and rightfully so. Better her than me.

"Are you going to let me in?"

"Not today."

"Come on, Ivy, this is ridiculous!"

This isn't how things were supposed to be, I know that. But I can't forfeit now, I can't let him win.

"Cara, put Dylan down for his nap, would you?" I ask, providing the instructions without taking my eyes off Sawyer, despite the fact that I have no idea when my son's nap time actually is.

"Are you sure, Mrs. Rogers?" Cara asks, adjusting my son on her hip.

I nod, the gesture more than enough to send her and Dylan up the stairs and out of earshot. The last thing I need is for Sawyer to set his sights on her. But he wastes no time laying into me, his eyes quickly shifting in anger as soon as Cara's gone. He points a threatening finger in my direction.

"See, *that*, right there is why you and I will never be 'You and I' again. You don't get to fuck my brother, pop out his kid, and then just expect me to be okay with it. We said no kids, remember?"

I feel it then, the shift between us. The notion that *his* word will be the final word, that he's putting his foot down and all is said and done, right here and now. I smile, a contortion I don't play with often enough these days, but it's there now.

My blood thrums from the alcohol, just the way I need it to. It does little to stop the anger from bubbling alongside it, though. I'm festering, I know this. It's like I'm walking too close to the edge of a cliff, well aware I'm going to slip and fall, but not giving a damn if I do.

I take a quick step back and slam the door, securing the deadbolt in place before stomping down the hall. It's cute, really, how Sawyer thinks he can walk away from all this unscathed, unharmed.

But he's on borrowed time.

He just doesn't know it yet.

JUST FOR YOU

Alisha

There's a certain feeling you get when you know the shoe is about to drop.

It's like a sudden pull in the atmosphere, a changing of the tides, a gut feeling that something big is coming. That it just might fix everything.

This battlefield we stand on is built on love, destroyed by it just the same. We're all just pawns in a life-sized game of chess, like tiny soldiers taking the first bullets on the front lines, and if we're lucky one of us will still be standing in the end.

There's no telling who it will be.

Roses are red
I watched as he bled
Violets are blue
I did it just for you

Ivy's latest declaration of love settles into my core.

This poem, this tiny piece of paper derived from fifty-seven letters to form seventeen words is the admission of guilt I've been waiting for. And it's the closest she'll ever come to a confession.

I read through it at least a hundred more times, soak up the meaning of the prose, the not-so-well hidden connotation buried within. I won't allow myself to make too much of it, I know I'm the only one who'll understand its value.

At least for me, these words bring closure. They give meaning to what I've put in motion, give me purpose again.

It's just a matter of time now.

The storm is coming.

PLANNED INTRUSION

Ivy

I'm hungover again.

Sawyer's impromptu visits tend to do that to me, regardless of how they turn out.

The fog in my head is thicker this time, but that isn't what startles me, what leaves me rooted to the kitchen chair, momentarily suspended in time. If I sit still long enough maybe the incessant knocker (banger) will take the hint and go away.

I haven't had enough caffeine to welcome this kind of raucous, and it doesn't help that Caramie doesn't seem to be around to answer the door.

What am I paying her for?

Do I answer it? Appease whoever feels the need to interrupt my morning so rudely? The banging continues; it looks like I'm getting up.

Against my will, I abandon my still-steaming cup of tea on the table and pull my robe closed before padding to the door. The flashing lights through the pained glass window stop me in my tracks.

They swarm through the foyer in a kaleidoscope of blue and red.

A set of uniformed officers stand perched on my doorstep, hands hovering over their holstered service weapons as they peer inside. Hesitantly, I take a step forward, unlocking the door and pulling it open just before the bigger of the two officers pounds on it again. His arm hovers in the air like he wasn't expecting me despite the planned intrusion.

"Do you mind?" I bark, my voice gravelly and thick with irritation.

"Are you Ivy Rogers?"

"Who's asking?"

"Officer Dettmund, ma'am," he gestures to the female officer beside him. "My partner, Officer Jarron. Are you Ivy Rogers?"

"Yes."

"Can you step outside, please?

"What for?"

"You're a person of interest in a cold-case. We'd like you to come to the station to answer a few questions."

"Wha—no." I shake my head vehemently. "No, you have the wrong house." I motion to slam the door in their faces, but a steel-toed boot blocks the way, a deep voice cuts through the tension.

"It's entirely your choice whether we take you in cuffs or not, ma'am, but this isn't an optional request." The politeness in his face from a moment ago is gone, replaced entirely by an all-business-don't-fuck-with-me facade.

My throat drops into my stomach.

I know what this is about.

But how?

How could they possibly know, and why are they here?

I stare in contention, my feet planted firmly to the hardwood floor, my heart hammering a beat in my chest. "May I get dressed first?"

"You can have some clothes delivered to you at the station. Is your purse nearby?" He peers into the foyer behind me and I lift my bag from the console table next to the door, attempting to clutch it to my chest. The officer pulls it away, takes a quick look inside.

"Any weapons in here?"

I shake my head and step out of the house and onto the concrete slab, the soft padding of Caramie's footsteps approaching behind me. The officer takes my arm; his hands are rough, but he's gentle when he guides me down the stoop and across the lawn as if he can't see the sidewalk.

Sawyer hates footprints in his lawn.

The cuffs go on despite my compliance, the metal clinking as its locked into position. I guess he was bluffing when he said the cuffs were optional.

"Ivy Rogers, you are under arrest for the murder of Erika Lacey. You have a right to remain silent..."

"Mrs. Rogers? What's going on? Whose Erika?" Caramie finally steps out of the house, my son attached to her hip. And because I know I won't be returning home anytime soon, I ask the one question worth asking at a moment like this.

"What do I need to do to grant temporary custody of my child to his nanny?"

"We can work that out down at the station," he says, turning to Caramie. "Miss, are you okay to maintain care of the child for the time being?"

Caramie nods reluctantly but says nothing as she hugs Dylan closer to her chest.

"Call my lawyer, Cara. Her information is in my address book in the office."

I suspect this must be traumatizing for her. But she just nods as if I'd told her I'll be home soon and asked her to have dinner on the table, maybe reminded her to pick up the dry cleaning.

Why isn't she more concerned right now?

I'm assisted into the back a squad car, my arms awkwardly bound behind my back so I can't even lean properly against the seat. The door closes and the officers take a moment to confer before separating and folding into their separate cruisers. Officer Dettmund, my apparent chauffeur, says nothing as he fastens his seatbelt. I catch his eyes in the rearview.

It's clear right away that he doesn't like me.

He pulls a pair of sunglasses over his eyes and enters something into the computer before putting the car in gear and steering it away from the curb. I turn and look through the rear window as we drive away, as my home becomes smaller, the two bodies on my front lawn seemingly shrinking into nothing.

An unexpected tear slides down my cheek.

I can't wipe it away because my hands are indisposed so it lands on my thigh.

But it's not my son's face that brings this wave of emotion, it's not the fact that the neighbors are watching and this is embarrassing beyond belief.

It's the look on Caramie's face that alarms me, and I don't know what this means for us. I don't know why it hurts so much or why I care that she's not in tears right now.

She's smiling as we drive away, holding a cell phone to her ear, my son still glued to her hip.

She certainly shouldn't be smiling at a time like this.

DECEPTIVELY CHARMING SOCIOPATH

THIS IS AWKWARD

Ivy

This is awkward.

I was really hoping you wouldn't find out about Erika. I feel like I've ruined things with you now, and that's really a shame because I thought we were off to such a good start, becoming friends and whatnot.

I've worked so hard to show you I'm a good person, that I'm not the monster Alisha has made me out to be, that Sawyer wants to prove I am.

See, the thing is, I left out a few things earlier. Omitted *some* of the truth, if you will. It's kind of a thing I do, I probably should have warned you. I'm not exactly proud of this oversight, but here we are. I do tell the truth more often than not, just not always the complete story, more of a partial tell really.

What I've told you *is* the truth.

I just left out some parts.

Contrary to what I told you before, my sister—*remember her?*—Erika was a royal pain in the ass. She was—*how do I say this politely?*—a manipulative bitch. Two-faced. Arrogant. We got along just fine when we were kids, that's why I said I grew up relatively *normal*.

But things change, as you know.

My little sister turned out to be a deceitful rat. I liked her less and less the older we got. She was a Daddy's girl, Mom's handy helper and their homegrown live-in spy. Erika criticized everything I did, and anytime I did something morally wrong in her eyes—which was often—she wasted no time running to Mom and Dad to tattled on her big sis.

They'd put her up to it too, not that either of them will ever admit to it.

But Erika was the reason I got grounded for shit I would've otherwise gotten away with. And it wasn't because I confided in her, I knew better than to do that. We hadn't been close in years, ever since she became the clear favorite in our household. No, it was because she was a lousy sister, with no respect to my privacy.

I found her going through my things all the time, reading diaries she shouldn't have been reading. She was good at finding ways to get into my hiding spots.

Those diaries were all I had, my private thoughts, and they were free reign to her once she ransacked my dresser drawers, my back pack. Anything to get me in trouble so *she* could stay on Mom and Dad's good graces. So she could get everything her little heart desired.

She was precious to them, could do no wrong, their little angel miracle baby that arrived a couple years after me. She was never supposed to be born in the first place.

And she hated to be reminded of that.

Now, you're probably over there thinking *that's no reason to kill your sister, Ivy.* And, you're right. I don't disagree. That's not why I killed her.

And I did, kill her, that is. No sense is beating around *that* proverbial bush. I simply had other, more pressing, reasons for doing it.

PRETENTIOUS TAPPING

Ivy

The interview room is small, a glorified closet if I'm doing it any justice.

I can't help but imagine Alisha in a room like this, maybe this exact one. I wonder if she found it as suffocating as I do right now.

Officer Dettmund—and the lady copy he's probably banging behind his wife's back—have officially turned me over to the homicide investigations team, or H.I.T. as they apparently prefer to be called. It doesn't sound very intimidating until you end up in my seat, a baseball bat's length away from a burly detective who's been investigating your sister's cold case for most of his adult life. Detective Wes Raylen they call him.

A tiger shark disguised as a teddy bear.

I cast my eyes downward and stare at the worn table, at the chipping plastic that's been picked at, prematurely aged by the anxious criminals who sat here before me. For a second I mull over how many of us have been in this seat, simultaneously terrified and excited at the same time.

Detective Raylen can't seem to sit still, like he's suffering from ADD or something. Not that I'd think less of him if he were, I'm sure he's a great detective. But I'm the one being put out here, not him. He doesn't get to play the annoyed party role, I do.

He taps a pen while he reads my case file, the beat likely mimicking whatever overplayed country song is stuck in his head this morning, but I don't listen to the radio often—certainly not to country—and can't seem to place it. He definitely looks like the kind of guy to enjoy today's latest and greatest hits; simple minded, a follower, not much of a leader.

Tap. Tap. Tip-pity tap.

The intimidation factor wears off the longer we sit here in silence; I'm not sure he realizes that, but if he reads any slower, surely I'll start to question his intellectual ability. And shouldn't he already be familiar with everything that file has to say?

"Should I come back at a later time?" I ask, disrupting his pretentious tapping. Not that I'm confident I have the option to stay or go, but at this point I'll say just about anything for a break in his rhythm.

He looks up and pushes the folder aside, leaving it open on the corner of the table before reaching for a Styrofoam cup on the other side. He slides it toward me as if demonstrating the definition of slow motion.

"For you," he says, his brows raising, hand motioning to the cup. "It's probably cold by now."

"You actually expect me to drink that?"

"Thought you might be thirsty."

Tap. Tap. Tap-pity tap.

"You thought wrong. Are we done here?"

"Quite the opposite, actually. I'm just getting started with you." He winks, and it's all I can do not to shudder. He's managed to reinstate his manliness with little effort, and now the room suddenly feels cold. Goosebumps prickle my skin despite the warm temperature and the moderate sweatshirt I've been gifted from the lost and found (since I've yet to receive the fresh set of clothes I was promised earlier). The cheap cotton material itches against my arms. "I need to know where you were the night of August 4, 2006," he says.

It's a statement, not a question, but it's clear he expects a definitive answer, which is the last thing I'll be giving him.

"How do you expect me to remember that? It was sixteen years ago."

"I would think it'd be pretty easy to remember, actually, seeing as it's the night your younger sister was *killed.* Most people would remember their exact whereabouts on a day like that."

"Hmm...ya know, come to think of it, you're right. I *should* be able to recall what I was doing the night my sister *died*, but..." I lean in real close, an accidental smirk playing on my lips, "...sorry, I don't."

"Mrs. Rogers, do you understand what kind of trouble you're in here?"

"I understand what kind of trouble you *think* I'm in, yes. But you're wasting your time, the taxpayer's hard-earned money. Don't you have better things to do than harass the family of a girl who's been dead for sixteen years?"

"That's odd."

"What?"

"The file I was just reading? You know, the new *evidence* that's come to light? Well, it seems to tell me a different story than what you're depicting here. That perhaps I'm not wasting my time—or the taxpayer's money—at all."

Sure, I'll bite.

"And what evidence would that be?"

"We'll get to that. First, tell me where you were that night. It's rather *important* to the narrative here."

"I don't recall."

"I have a feeling you do."

"Yeah? Do you like to talk about your feelings, detective? Sounds to me like you'd make a great therapy patient. Maybe you should see someone."

Tap. Tap.

"It's just interesting to me, you know?" he continues. "That I would tell you there's new evidence in your sister's case, and you immediately ask what the evidence is as if you know there's evidence to be found."

"What's your point?"

"My point is that you should either be excited or scared by this new evidence. You know, depending on your level of innocence, whether you give a shit. But you seem a bit nonchalant about it. Aloof, if you will."

"Yeah, well, she and I didn't get along the greatest. What can I say? I came to terms with her death years ago; I don't need to relive it."

"Well, I'd like to be able to offer your parents some justice, wouldn't you?"

Tap. Tap. Tip-pity-tap-tap.

My butt hole puckers at the mention of my parents, and just like that, this conversation is officially over. My arms fold across my chest and I lean back in the seat, prepared to sweat it out on mute for the duration of the interrogation.

I refuse to discuss those assholes.

"I'd like to call my lawyer now."

And there he goes with the tapping again.

A QUICK FUCK WILL HELP

Sawyer

Ivy's arrest is a bit shocking, to be honest. I can't say I didn't see it coming, but she's always been so good at staying under the radar, playing the system. Nearly five years together and here, I had no idea my wife had a sister. That her parents hadn't been killed in a car crash as she'd previously stated. She'd told such a convincing story.

Always so clever, that Ivy.

Imagine my surprise when the faces of her loving parents—Sebastien and Cristina Lacey, their names—flash across my television screen.

Not just in picture either, but in motion.

Speaking.

Crying.

Very much alive.

"We just want justice for our daughter."

I really should have looked more closely into my wife's background, I see that now, recognize my mistakes. How unlike me not to cover my bases, to protect myself. I trusted her with blind ambivalence.

Maybe I *am* an idiot after all.

The pieces will fall where they may, I suppose. She's dug her own grave, I just may have handed her the shovel. The past does tend to catch up with us sooner or later.

It's likely, I suppose, that I'll be making another court appearance in the near future; there's no way whatever expensive law firm she hires won't want to have a chat with me, her legally bound husband.

Not that I have information to share.

These thoughts flutter through my mind while I work on tonight's dinner, the television still set to the local news station as I prepare salmon and wild rice with asparagus. My lady-friend should be arriving any minute now, so I need to get my mind off my wife and her extracurriculars.

But I've burnt the salmon.

The rice is overcooked, the asparagus still raw.

This news is just too mind boggling, and it's taking a minute to sink in. When my date finally knocks on the door, it's so soft I barely hear it, but I abandon the burnt fish on the stove and punch the power button on the remote to turn off the TV and dissolve the images of my previously presumed dead in-laws.

I need tonight, this company.

A quick fuck should help me relax.

It always does.

I turn the deadbolt and pull the door open. For some reason she looks hotter today than usual, more...grown up, sophisticated. And I must admit, it's nice. Sure, she's a little young for me, but she's damn good in the sack and, surprisingly, a near perfect partner in crime despite my initial apprehensions.

What more could a guy ask for?

"Hi, baby," she says, stepping inside and delivering a peck on my cheek. "You took forever to let me in. Is everything okay?"

"Yes, sorry. I was cooking dinner." I flash a smile, tell myself to shake off the thoughts roaming through my head, and take in the sight of her.

My new mistress.

At her long, toned legs in those black stiletto heels, the curve of her ass beneath her khaki coat. From the looks of it, there's not much under there and she officially has my attention.

"Oh, how sweet, Grant! You didn't have to..."

Why she still calls me Grant, I have no idea. She knows my real name, has since the beginning. It's just a thing between us I suppose. I can't say I mind, really. I feel less like Sawyer every day as it is.

That life seems to be behind me, preserved for nothing more than the memories that came of it.

"Yeah, well, it's uh—it's burnt, the salmon. So...we can't eat it." She pouts, and somehow it's sexy despite it's childish connotation. But she recovers quickly, untying the belt of her trench coat and sliding it off her shoulders. It drops to the ground, and my God, she's beautiful. All innocence is lost at the sight of her in *that* little number. It's sheer lace, everywhere but between her legs.

Just like the outfits Alisha used to wear for me.

Yes, a quick fuck will definitely do.

***

"I assume you've seen the news?" she asks, dismounting me. She rolls onto her back, pulling the covers up to her torso, but leaving her tits exposed. I reach over and work a perky nipple through my fingers, my heart rate steadily decreasing. It always takes a moment to come down from the high of her.

"Right before you arrived, actually. That's how I managed to screw up dinner."

She giggles at my expense, and it's adorable the way her nose crinkles up. "You're quite the little investigator," I tell her.

She knows what the headlines said, the accusations behind them and what this means for me. For my wife now that the world knows she's a killer.

"It wasn't hard," she admits with a wink. "The woman is almost *never* home, and when she is, she's usually passed out in her bedroom with the door locked. Hardly sees her kid—don't even get me started there."

"I can't say I'm surprised. She never wanted to settle down."

She rolls onto her side, burrowing under my arm and bringing a soft hand to my chest. "Trust me, babe, this will all work out. We did good."

"I have no doubt you'll make sure of it," I say. With my hand on her chin, I pull her to me and bring my lips to hers. Her lipstick is smudged, the remnants of the cherry red still trailing down my chest from our first go around.

"Round two already?" she asks, lifting the sheet and taking a peek at the tent I'm re-erecting.

I'm hard, what can I say?

It's the way she works those fingernails on my stomach, the playfulness in her eyes, the twitch of her upper lip. Maybe even the idea that this woman is nearly fifteen years younger than me and I can keep up with her, please her the way she deserves to be pleased.

Or perhaps it's the excitement of knowing she helped me put my wife behind bars.

The fact that she didn't ask any questions when I told her what I needed her to do.

"See what you do to me?" I growl and she pulls me on top of her this time, yelping below me when I bring my mouth to her nipple and nibble it with my teeth. I can't help but moan myself when she grips my cock in her hand, wasting no time as she guides me to her, still very wet, center.

And I know I shouldn't do it, but I close my eyes, and for just a second I'm almost convinced it's not her I'm inside of. I shake the thought away, guilt gnawing at me from the inside.

This is not the time to be thinking about Alisha.

Not when this woman has done so much for me.

It's amazing what a woman will do for a little cash though, isn't it? Stability often comes at a price, and she was willing to pay it, to go along with the plan I'd laid out before her. That's what this is about, after all: a plan.

Because my wife was a liability.

A wrinkle in an otherwise crisp bed sheet.

And who better to help me take her out of the picture than the nanny I delivered right to her doorstep? I just didn't think we'd end up in bed together, me and Caramie, but I guess we can chalk that one up as a perk of the job, hmm?

Oh, yes, she's definitely a perk of the job.

FIVE-STAR NANNY

Sawyer

Now, I know what you're thinking—I shouldn't be sleeping with my wife's twenty-five-year-old nanny, yeah, yeah. I'm a pig and I shouldn't have gotten involved because it couldn't possibly do any of us any good. Right? Am I close? Getting warmer?

I thought so.

But you don't know the whole story. It's not your fault, surely, you couldn't have seen this coming. See, the thing is, sometimes the obvious answer is right under your nose.

Sometimes the only way to keep the enemy close is to give them exactly what they want.

Fun fact: I've known Caramie a lot longer than my wife has.

In fact, Ivy has *me* to thank for her five-star nanny.

Of course, my intentions for bringing the two of them together were not good. Not in your eyes, anyway. But it needed to be done. Cara works for *me*—or *worked* for me, I should say, as my office manager at the firm. She didn't last long, not for lack of skill set, mind you; she performed the duties of the job just fine.

I simply saw potential in her, needed her for bigger and better things.

It was easy to see, that she was more than capable of playing a much larger role in my continued success. From inside my estranged wife's home instead of the desk outside my office.

It helped that she's so easy on the eyes. The flirting between us started right away, within the first week if I remember correctly, and it wasn't long after that we were fucking on top of my desk in between meetings. We're a classic grumpy/sunshine story, Cara and I, but that's not what's important here.

The important thing was not to get caught.

It was planned before Ivy had the baby, while she was pregnant and doing everything she could to get me to stay. But I'd already moved out, started seeing Cara after hours and things spiraled from there. There was a lot on the line for me; my reputation at the office didn't need the kind of scrutiny that follows an office affair. And Caramie certainly deserved better than to look like a home-wrecker should the news travel back to the wrong party.

But she knew my predicament, how Ivy wanted to ruin me.

She offered to help, and I told her how she could. I'd earned her trust, then enticed her with some money. And that's when the plan came together.

Like I said, I didn't think she'd be so quick to jump on board, but she was all in. Ready and willing to help me cut ties with my wife for good. To take her out of the game even though I knew she'd go down swinging.

By the time Ivy had the baby, we were ready. The plan was in motion; Cara had been let go from the firm (things *just didn't work out*), and we'd put together her profile on the nanny finder website.

Which is why she's now employed by my wife, which technically means I'm the one paying her, but it's legit on paper, despite our cruel intentions.

She even got a pay bump and a place to stay. I needed her eyes inside of my house, to watch Ivy, to watch the safe in my office until I could get in there and empty it out. I'd left so quickly when shit hit the fan that I didn't take much with me. I wasn't able to get the safe cleared, and there was useful information in there.

And that's where Cara initially came in.

The plan was for her to work for Ivy for a bit, and when she'd had enough of Ivy's bullshit, she'd quit. It was simple, sure, but believable considering the source. My wife is not an easy woman to get along with, as you may have figured out.

The thing is, I didn't necessarily trust her with the safe yet. I couldn't bring myself to give her the key code right off the bat. She needed to prove herself first, show me she could pull off the illusion.

It wasn't long before I realized Cara was nothing like Ivy. She wasn't about to screw me over. In fact, Caramie came up with a better idea, something that would work a even more in our favor, give us a little more bang for our buck.

Why not have her work for Ivy a little longer and see what she could dig up on her while I wasn't around? I knew our divorce would be messy, I just didn't know *how* messy it'd be and I wanted a bigger insurance policy.

Ivy expected alimony, and a bite off my trust fund despite five-year marriage clause and the fact that she had another man's baby. Her lawyer was working on a way around that, apparently, as confirmed by Cara last week. Ivy thinks she's entitled to everything, but she's not. I just have to make sure she doesn't find a loophole; there's always a loophole. I mean, the woman hasn't worked a day in her life, but somehow she'd be entitled to *my* money, even once we split? Sorry, but really? No fucking thank you.

Caramie's plan was brilliant, it really was.

We'd build a case against her. Prove to a judge—if necessary—that Ivy's extracurricular activities made her not just an adulterer, but an unfit mother.

See, Ivy was working for Lady Ann again, and this time she wasn't keeping things kosher by any means. She didn't know I knew about her prior affiliation with the escort agency either, but the things is, I'm pretty resourceful when I need to be; I was more than well aware of her transgressions in the bowels of that brothel.

What I hadn't expected, was that she'd return to work for Lady Ann once we'd split, after Alisha's trial. I guess rejection will do that to a person, but who am I to judge?

It was Cara who thought well enough to share some additional information with me, when she started to question Ivy's whereabouts, her frequent absences at home.

"She leaves every night around seven and doesn't return until morning most days," she'd said.

"Where does she go?"

"I don't know, she's never said one way or the other, but she usually looks a little...disheveled...when she strolls in the next morning."

"Is she seeing someone?" An unexpected bout of jealously slithered in my stomach as I asked, but I ignored it, told myself it didn't matter.

"Not that I know of."

I knew Cara would come through for me, I did. Her obsession with my cock bodes well for me in more ways than one, and well, can you blame her? She's dedicated, let's just say that.

But I had no idea she would uncover what she uncovered, what she'd find.

She's even brighter than I gave her credit for.

And it'll come to light, very soon it will.

"We should follow her. See what she's up to," I suggested. My curiosity was more than piqued; I needed to know what my estranged wife was up to.

"How am I supposed to do that when I'm taking care of her kid all the time?"

"Oh, that's easy."

She raised a brow, the obvious answer not quite there for her yet. "We hire a babysitter," I said.

"*I'm* the babysitter."

"Right. But who says you can't babysit Ivy instead?"

So, we played house. Cara brought baby Dylan to my place and together we pretended to be the doting mother and father in desperate need of some time out of the house. We interviewed a few local teenagers looking to make some extra cash.

Then we hired one.

And we followed Ivy to Lady Ann's that night. Straight to the place where it all began, but of course, I neglected to let Cara in on that little secret, that I had ties to the place, too.

She waited in the car, on look out in case Ivy came out while I was inside. Really, it was more of a way for me to maintain my cover; people would recognize me in there, they'd know who I was. Hell, I still had the credentials to get in, too.

I put Cara on camera duty. She stayed busy securing the evidence while I made my way inside. Masquerade night, to my surprise. The easiest events to get into, and subsequently back out of should anything go wrong.

Once I was inside I made my way around the rooms in search of my darling wife, hopeful she didn't spot me in the sea of sex addicts among us. It was clear within minutes that Lady Ann had found some more lucrative ways to run her business in the time since I'd been gone. Security had been upgraded, the women sexier than ever, more daring, more bedroom doors intentionally left open. The men were going from room to room, taking their turns without reprimand.

And I tried to resist, I did.

But my cock was hard, fighting against the zipper of my trousers, and there was little I could do to stop myself from participating once the arousal hit me.

I managed to find the room, the one she was in.

I watched her.

She looked stunning as always; orgasms had a tendency to do that to her, bring light to her eyes. Dark corners do a gawker like me wonders in that place, let me tell you. It was easy to hide in the shadows, to observe. The hidden camera in my masquerade mask captured all the ammo I needed.

And once I had her face on video, her transgressions documented from inside the house, the deal was done.

With the camera switched off, I saw myself out of the room and entered another, this time releasing my cock from my pants and taking a turn on a blonde in a pair of black leather boots.

The only thing I did that Ivy didn't bother to do that night was close the door.

I shoved my guilt aside, proud of my night's work. Cara would be none the wiser to my little mishap, and with the video evidence I'd captured, surely no judge in the world would grant Ivy alimony after witnessing proof of her illicit affairs, right?

I had her.

WE GOT BOOBS

Ivy

I had a best friend once. I imagine that's a little hard to believe, perhaps it sounds a little fictional given what you've learned about me, but it's true. Her name was Joy, and she was the very definition of the word. A bright light in my otherwise dark world.

In the grand scheme of things, I suppose our friendship wasn't all that life-changing, but back then? Back then it felt like we were destined to be friends forever, attached at the hip and I pictured us old and senile in our rockers, still causing trouble into our old age.

We'd been inseparable since kindergarten, having been assigned as table partners and decided that meant we had to do everything else together, too. Joy came from a good home—an *actual* good home, not the kind I pretended to be from—and she was an only child without the cliched spoiled rich girl attitude to go along with the title. The Tiernan family was the epitome of every 90s sitcom ever written.

And I wanted in.

I spent as much time at the Tiernan household as I could. Joy and I baked cookies with her mom on Sundays, and I often tagged along to family outings. Valley Fair, shopping trips to the Mall of America, the Minnesota State Fair, movie nights, day trips to one of Minnesota's ten thousand lakes. It didn't matter where, as long as I didn't have to be at home with my own family.

Joy felt more like a sister to me than Erika ever did, and that meant something in my book.

In sixth grade we both got boobs.

In ninth grade we shared our first cigarette (and hated it).

In eleventh grade she got her first boyfriend and later that year, I got drunk and had sex with him at a party. We vowed never to tell her, promised each other it was a one-time thing and would never happen again.

The thing is, I was upset, hurt.

I'd been rejected and I didn't know what to do with that.

I kissed Joy.

Earlier that week. It was stupid and I don't know why I did it. I knew I shouldn't have, but I did it; I couldn't take it back and it ruined our friendship. Joy didn't understand, she didn't feel what I felt when I looked at her. She wasn't curious like I was.

She wasn't confused.

My lips were on hers and I never wanted to break them apart. But her palms pressed heavily against my chest as she shoved me away. Like she had no idea who I was and why I was there.

"Gross, Ivy! Why would you do that?" she'd barked in disgust, literally wiping the taste of me from her lips, smearing her lipstick onto the sleeve of her sweater.

"I'm so sorry," was all I could think to say. She was crying then, actually *crying*, the tears streaming down her cheeks like someone who'd lost their Grandmother.

A person should never cry like that over a kiss.

A kiss is supposed to be a happy moment, like fireworks in the summertime.

But she cried, and that made everything worse, the embarrassment, the shame, was all too much.

It hit me then, the reality of the situation. The finality of our friendship after so many years. My best friend was homophobic. How had I let that fact slip by? I should have known, should have seen the warning signs, but I was too immersed in her to notice.

"Don't ever talk to me again!"

And just like that, she was gone. Joy had been sucked from my life, eliminated, all because I couldn't keep my stupid feelings to myself. Our friendship, the memory of her and all the firsts we'd shared, would forever be tarnished.

That should have been the end of it.

But it wasn't, not by a long shot.

Because it was later that week, at Savvy Drayer's Valentine's party, that I saw her again. We locked eyes across the room, and she glared at me with such disdain that I couldn't look away. I saw something change in her eyes.

It didn't help that she was there with *my* sister, my bratty fifteen-year-old sister who was supposed to be at home writing a paper for her Government class. They stood there together, watching me, both of them giggling behind cupped hands as they sipped from their Solo cups and shared secrets that weren't theirs to share.

I balled my fists, squeezed tightly so the fingernails left little crescent moons on my palms. The pain was good, necessary, because without it I didn't feel human.

I needed to feel human.

That's when I went upstairs to find Trevor, the aforementioned boyfriend.

I didn't think, just took him by the hand and drug him into an empty bedroom. He didn't ask questions, didn't harbor any more remorse than I did, so what did we have to lose?

The sex was quick, sloppy and awkward as it always is at that age. But I'd done what I set out to do. I took my revenge and I'd do whatever I needed to do with it when the time came.

They continued dating until evidence of our betrayal found its way to the internet later that summer. Somehow, overnight I became the star of a show I didn't know I was performing in, and my do-no-wrong sister was both the director and producer.

That's right, my own flesh and blood sold me out and uploaded a video of me having sex with my best friend's boyfriend onto the internet.

She'd followed me, us, into that bedroom, and recorded the whole thing on her flip phone through a crack in the door.

Erika was smart about it, too.

She held onto that video clip for months, somehow managing to keep it a dirty little secret until she saw just the right opportunity and took it.

That's when it all started really, the beginning of the end.

When I made the decision to kill my sister.

That sex tape didn't just expose my most intimate moments (and body parts), it exposed my sister's true colors, her ill-intent. She was more dangerous than she looked.

She was the enemy.

Before school started in the fall, my Senior year, the entire school had seen the video, probably even saved it to their desktop computers, their flash drives. The eyes could not unsee.

Same went for my parents.

And Trevor's, and Joy's, and the school principal. The list

goes on and on.

I no longer had a best friend.

I no longer had a sister.

And unlike Trevor who was high-fived by his chauvinistic friends and only mildly reprimanded by his parents (because, hey, *we're just glad you didn't get her pregnant*), I was ruined.

Disowned by every single person I knew, including my parents. Grounded for the foreseeable future, likely until I turned eighteen, even longer if I chose to stick around.

The only thing left on my mind after that was revenge.

My sister was going to pay for what she had done.

I'd known long before then that Erika had a problem, that her soul was no less dark than my own. Her heart had filled with hate long before mine did, so I like to think she had it coming in the end.

She did this to herself.

DEAR DIARY

Ivy

It never does take much for a sane person to come unhinged. Not much at all. The screw can wiggle loose right under your nose and you won't even realize it until it's too late. A snide comment can be made softly under someone's breath, a dirty look shot in your direction. If done at just the wrong moment, watch out.

I don't recall the exact moment I snapped. I *want* to—I think it could be helpful to know—but I don't. All I can say is that one day I was okay, and one day I wasn't. I could sit here and blame any number of things like I tend to do, but the truth is, deep down I always knew something was *off*, that I could lose it at any moment.

I could feel it in my bones.

There was a storm brewing, and I was ready to unleash it.

The cloud had hovered for far too long.

The dam was bound to break eventually.

And it did.

It broke, and there's one hell of a crack in the facade.

They've found something, the police.

I don't know what, but it feels big, maybe even monumental.

They've brought me back in for questioning, out of the cest pool that is the county jail, for what I imagine will be another several hours of curious word play.

I can't say I'm in the mood for any more today.

Jail is exhausting. Nobody really tells you that, that it's mind-numbingly boring to the point of exhaustion and by the time you realize it, it's too late. You're there and you can't leave no matter what you do, who you know.

Detective Raylen finally joins me and my lawyer, Kelly Moon, in the interview room, his usual smug expression plastered on his face. He carries in a white file box labeled with black Sharpie, my name and case number scribbled on the side of it.

I'd think it were a scare tactic, just an empty box for show, if it didn't make such a thump when he set it down.

"Care to explain these?" he asks, opening the cardboard lid and pulling several books out of it. It takes a moment to sink in, to realize what he's holding in his hands, but when I do, I can't hold back my surprise. The sharp intake of breath, the hand to my chest.

They found my diaries.

I'd like to say I'm baffled, shocked even, but I'm not. It's a surprise to see them after all the time they've been missing, but the fact that they've come into the possession of the police isn't that unexpected considering. Sure, I'd have locked them in the safe if I'd known they were on to me, but that opportunity never presented itself. I was preoccupied; it all happened so fast.

Sawyer.

He's the only explanation, really. He would know where to look, was well aware of all the little nooks and crannies of the home we once shared. I wonder how long he's had them.

"I didn't even know you kept a diary," he'd said when I asked him if he'd seen them.

It had to be him.

Fuck.

I've written some questionable things in those diaries—damning things. And it's all in the wrong hands now. The proof in the pudding.

I know I should say something now, but the words are lodged behind my lips, stuck like taffy on the roof of my mouth and all I can do is savor their flavor before I eventually swallow them.

"Mrs. Rogers, I asked you a question," Raylen says, pulling the first book from the pile and running his fingers along the colored tabs sticking out of the pages. He flips to a yellow tab, exposing one of hundreds, maybe thousands, of private entries in a book I wrote but never intended to share.

"I heard you," I finally mutter.

There, I've said something. I'm not mute after all.

"Great. And?"

"And...I didn't realize you were such a book nerd."

"I'm not. But I did find this one rather interesting," he taunts, waving the book in front of him. "I'll read you a passage."

"That's not necessary."

"Oh, I think it is. Unless you'd rather summarize it for me? I'm sure Kelly will be interested in what we've found here. You may be familiar with the content, though, yes?"

"Why do you ask a question when you already know the answer?"

"So, you *do* know what these are then? I don't need to explain them to you, read them verbatim until we're all blue in the face?" Raylen's eyes roam the room and I see Kelly make eye contact with him before writing something in her notebook.

She knows I'm guilty now, any doubt she may have had is surely gone now that my diaries have been exposed.

It probably changes things, but she has to defend me anyway. I'll remind her of that if I have to, can't let her forget who she's working for, can I?

It's slow, but I shake my head no in response to Raylen's final question.

The wheels in my head turn rapidly.

There's no positive way to spin this.

I'm fucked.

Ivy Rogers Diary Entry

September 4, 2004, Age 17

It's hard to say what normal is anymore. Were we all born "normal", only for some of us to later turn insane, or did a select group of us just start out this way? Maybe the beast festers all along, ready to awaken at any given moment, for any given reason.

Maybe there's one inside of all of us.

I like to think so anyway.

The thought is oddly comforting, but I'm not sure why.

Mom says I have too many mean bones in me, that sometimes they break. I don't think that's a thing, but I overheard her say that to Dad last night after I was sent away from the dinner table. My attitude, apparently, wasn't on their agenda for the evening. And that's fine, I don't care. She's a shitty cook anyway and I'll just sneak out to McD's or something after they go to bed.

But it's all bullshit, because Erika's attitude was way worse than mine and she wasn't asked to leave, so I think that tells me all I need to know.

She was at that party too, fucked in the head just enough to capture my sexual activities on camera, then later to share them with the world.

Not that she suffered much in terms of consequences, not the way I did. She wasn't summoned to her bedroom for all hours of the day, no phone, no TV, no computer. It's like they wanted to reward her for catching me in the act.

Like they were proud of her because at least she knew what I was doing was wrong.

See, nothing ever changes around here. It doesn't matter how hard I try to show them, to help them see that she *is the problem.*

It's fucked up, but sometimes I think about killing her.

There. I said it. I've been holding that in for a while now, but I can't do it anymore. I just can't.

It's...I dunno, weird, to think that way, right? I know it is, but it's true and you're only supposed to write true things in a diary, so that's what I'm trying to do here. It's not like anyone is ever going to read this.

I think I could do it, though. Kill my sister. I never miss her when she's gone, and wouldn't care less if she got hurt. One time she broke her wrist playing kick ball in gym class. It was a few years ago, looked super gnarly, but also kinda cool. Anyway, she was a cry baby about it and all I wanted to do was break the other one, too. I mean, who breaks their wrist, of all things, playing kick ball?

Those next few weeks afterward were a nightmare. Mom made me do everything for her, short of wiping her ass; luckily it was the other wrist that broke. But they even bought her a little bell, and fuck her for using it so religiously.

Fuck them for making me tend to her needs.

Here's the thing, I'm done playing nice. I can't do this anymore. I can't sit here and let her rule the roost forever.

I have to do something.

And I think we're all capable of something *big, something seemingly unimaginable. Maybe it's not as unimaginable as we think. Maybe society just wants us to think it is.*

Anger is normal.

Fear is normal.

Maybe the urge to kill is, too.

The decision to protect your own life above all others? It's primal. Instinctual. Animals do it every day; all the nature programs tell us that. So, if it's okay for animals, why can't it be okay for humans?

Maybe we just need to normalize it somehow, every he, she, they, them, and child for themselves.

The weak ones will fall first.

Like Erika.

She's my prey and I'm the hunter now.

She won't even smell me coming.

SHIT STORM

Sawyer

I knew about the diaries.

Of course I did, a man knows what goes on in his own home, even when it looks like he doesn't. It was a while ago, though, when I found them, probably a few years. I didn't bother to read them at the time, that was my mistake. I really could have ended this a lot sooner had it not been for my laziness. I was distracted with other things, what can I say?

I should have known there'd be something newsworthy within those pages.

Who in their right mind stumbles upon the innermost thoughts of *the* Ivy Rogers and doesn't bother to take a peek at those words?

An idiot, that's who.

Deep down I must have known. Maybe I wasn't ready to learn what she was hiding. I always knew there was something, but this? Definitely not what I imagined. All I knew at the time of my discovery was that those diaries would be useful someday. That's why I hid them under the floorboards in our room instead of returning them to her. She'd been looking for them for a while, was frustrated that she lost them, but I knew I'd give them a read eventually, maybe take a gander once things settled down a bit. I wasn't ready to give them back.

But I had other shit to do, like make nice with the leader of an organized crime ring.

I had a pay day to secure.

The diaries slipped my mind until recently, until this shit storm with Ivy started blowing in and I needed some reassurance, a way to make sure my wife kept her nose out of my affairs. It was Caramie who came through for me, though. Those diaries and proof of my ties with the Ehrens-Havenbrook Corporation were the smoking gun in that house after I left, the damning evidence I needed to regain possession of.

And my lover—the nanny to my wife's illegitimate son—was more than willing to retrieve them for me. She came in hot with the ace of spades in the last hand, she did.

I won't need her much longer, but part of me thinks I should keep her around, see what else she brings to the table. The thing is, I'm not sure what else she's good for yet, but she's loyal, I'll give her that.

The words feel hollow even as I say them. I know I'm a douche, but hey, I never said I was a nice guy.

Surely you know this, too.

But if this doesn't work, if I can't make Ivy go away and stay on Connor Ehrens's good graces at the same time, I may have to resort to more permanent measures, call in a few favors.

The last thing I need is my wife spilling secrets.

You don't mess with Connor Ehrens and his business, you just don't. The man has killed for much less and let's just say I wouldn't want to meet him in a dark alley after crossing him, if you know what I mean.

Besides, the way I see it?

I've done my wife a favor.

With any luck, she may just end up right where she wants to be.

BUT WAIT, THERE'S MORE

Ivy

I'm uncomfortable with the knowledge that my diaries are now under a microscope, spread open for anyone and their mother to do with what they please. Detective Raylen has left the room and I sit here now with my lawyer, likely for another umpteen hours.

And Kelly Moon is fiery this afternoon, let me tell you. I knew she was scrappy before she even opened her mouth. The business suit she's wearing today looks like it was made for her, the way it's tailored to hug her curves without over-sexualizing her is impressive.

I don't want to need her, but I do. Raylen's claws are in deep and I'm not sure I can stop the bleeding on my own.

Not to say that I like her or anything, but her services are necessary so here we are.

"The State has brought forth some additional evidence, Ivy—can I call you *Ivy*? Mrs. Rogers still feels a little channel-two-ish."

I nod, careful not to chuckle and give her the impression that I'm enjoying our scheduled girl time. "What evidence?"

"I assume you were unaware you were being filmed?"

Her words cut like a knife to my gut. I can only assume she's talking about *before*—about my armature porn debut from high school, but the look on her face tells me otherwise.

This is something new.

"*What?* When?"

"Do you work for an escort service called Lady Ann?"

Oh no.

"Excuse me?"

"Do you?"

"What's it to you?" Her face softens at my rebuttal and I almost feel bad for snapping at her, but to be honest, I'm getting a little sick of random evidence finding its way into our discussions.

"I'm your lawyer, Ivy," Kelly says. "That means I'm in your corner and you should at least try to be honest with me. I don't care what you *actually* did, I'm just here to make sure you don't end up spending the rest of your life in prison."

Fair enough.

Kelly Moon: 1

Ivy Rogers: 0

"So, I'll ask you one more time. Do you work for an escort service called Lady Ann?"

"Yes."

"I thought so." She reaches into an oversize satchel and pulls out a stack of documents, sliding them over to me one at a time, before leaning back in her seat and folding her arms across her chest.

It takes a moment for it to sink, what she's showing me.

Pictures.

Surveillance photos.

Of me.

At Lady Ann's.

Where no cameras or cell phones are allowed.

"Look familiar?" she asks.

I nod with apprehension, but it's not the pictures that render me speechless, that increase my heart rate and threaten to send me into a full blown panic attack.

It's the flash drive she's holding between her fingers.

There's more.

"This," she starts, waving it tauntingly in the air, "is your new worst enemy. Any guesses what's on it?"

It only takes me one.

But she's wrong.

These videos aren't my new worst enemy.

Unlike me, Kelly Moon doesn't know what's in those diaries.

"Were you aware you were being recorded?"

"No."

So, here I am involved in yet another sex tape scandal. *How did this happen*, one might wonder. I can't overlook the irony; a sex tape started all this, I suppose it'll end it, too.

It's almost more unexpected this time around.

I had no idea these recordings existed outside of the ones I took part in willingly, the ones Sawyer and I made together, but these aren't from Sawyer's personal collection. I'd recognize those, and he's in them, too, so there'd be no point in sharing them since they'd ruin him, too.

These are new.

Recent.

Taken at Lady Ann's sometime *after* I resumed my employment. From the looks of it, just a few weeks ago.

And this time, there's more at stake for me, this time I have so much more to lose. And I wouldn't mind, really. If it weren't for my son and the trust fund, and the fact that I'm determined to get my hands on that money.

All this time, and Sawyer still found a way to back me into a corner.

I just don't know how.

Or better yet, *why* these videos matter in the grand scheme of things.

It has literally nothing to do with the fact that my sister is dead.

So why am I being questioned about them?

MOTHER DEAREST

Ivy

My first appearance is today.

In court, in front of the judge.

It's bittersweet, this formality, but in a way I welcome it. It's time to set things in motion, get this show on the road. I'm tired of sitting around waiting for what happens next.

First degree murder.

It sounds so official, so permanent.

Like there's no way out of this no matter how I spin it.

But all they have are my diaries, circumstantial evidence at best, right? What can they really prove with those words?

Anyone could have written them.

The videos of me at Lady Ann's mean nothing in relation to my case, merely a show of character I can easily talk my way around. Surely they won't do any damage when all is said and done, they're just a scare tactic. I'm a sex worker, so what?

That doesn't prove I'm a murderer.

It's simply an unfortunate coincidence.

I stand now, with Kelly at the defense table, my wrists shackled to my waist, hands shaking. The clink of the chains giving me away despite the confidence I have that I'll be going ough, in my opinion. How I have to sit nge jumpsuit, chained together like an tch my own nose with ease. If criminals ven guilty, why don't they at least let us wear our ow[illegible] to these things?

I *look* like a criminal today.

Hell, I feel like one, too.

First time for everything, I guess.

"All rise...the honorable Judge John Waskey presiding."

Well, he doesn't look so bad, this judge. Just a regular old guy in a fancy robe, probably somebody's grandfather, a damn fine Canasta player.

I like to think so, anyway.

The courtroom is seated, Kelly and I included, and I can't help but wish I had something to drink. She warned me about this, the scratchy throat and how nervous people get once they're in the hot seat.

"The Court will now call the State of Minnesota vs. Ivy Jean Rogers, case number..."

Judge Waskey clears his throat and shifts briefly in his chair. At the sound of his voice he's no longer someone's grandfather, but rather the next man I aim to please. Not that I have any clue how I'll do that in this getup, but nonetheless, I find myself sitting up a little straighter, smiling, doing my best to look like an innocent offender. "Parties, please state your appearances," he says.

"May it please the Court, the State appears by Scott Pender."

"May it please the Court, Ms. Rogers appears in person and with her attorney, Kelly Moon."

So formal, they sound.

This is weird.

It hits me then, the seriousness of all this. The fact that everyone in this courtroom already thinks I'm guilty. There's a certain look in their eyes now, a distrust of sorts.

"We are here for a first appearance in this matter. In this complaint Ms. Rogers, you are charged with one count of murder in the first degree. Do you understand what you are charged with in this case?"

"Yes, your Honor," I state with as much conviction as I can muster. I want to say more, claim my innocence, but Kelly insists this isn't the time for that.

"Judge, we ask that the defendant be released on their own recognizance. Ms. Rogers has no prior criminal history, and is a pillar of the community. She and her husband donate thousands per year to the Minnesota Community Foundation, amongst other charitable giving. She has stable housing, financial means, and will be happy to await trial from the comfort of her home, where she can remain with her young son."

"State?"

"Judge, the State feels that Ms. Rogers is not only a flight risk, but a danger to the community. She is charged with murder in the first degree, which carries a life sentence, if convicted. We would ask that bond be set in the amount of one million dollars."

Fuck you, Scott Pender. A million dollars? Is he serious?

It's quiet for a moment, as Judge Waskey makes his considerations. I don't expect it, the words that come from his mouth next, and I sure hope Kelly's paying attention because once he drops the first bomb, I don't hear the rest.

"Given the nature of the crime, bail is set today at one million

dollars...”

***

I find myself in the visitor’s center the next morning, fully expecting to see Sawyer or even Caramie sitting in the chair across from me, preferably letting me know my bail is being paid and that I’ll be released soon.

I can’t wait to wash the stench of this place off, take a hot bath, drink a bottle of wine.

But it’s neither of their faces I see when I walk in there, it’s not their eyes looking back at me when I reach for the phone on the wall.

It’s my mother’s.

That’s right, *the* Cristina Lacey is here in the flesh, finally reuniting with the daughter she wishes she never had. And she doesn’t look happy, not one bit.

Not that I blame her.

Sixteen years have passed since I last saw her face. Sixteen years since I’ve heard her voice, or felt the string of the accusations in her eyes. I almost can’t believe she’s here, but then again, she’d go anywhere—do *anything*—for her precious Erika, wouldn’t she?

So, of course she’s here.

I suck in a breath and take a tentative seat across from her; I don’t envision this going well, so I’m not sure how long I’ll sit with her, or why I do at all. She hasn’t earned the right to speak to me, not after all this time. I know I should turn around and head back to my holding cell, pull an Alisha and refuse to see her.

But for some reason I don’t.

For some reason, I suddenly want nothing more than to hear my mother's voice.

We reach for the phone at the same time, placing the plastic receivers to our ears, our heads unknowingly tilting at the same time, in the same direction.

Like mother, like daughter.

"Ivy."

She says my name and it sounds weird on her lips, tastes bitter like an overripe grapefruit. I spot the tears in her eyes, but I know she wants to hold them back more than anything.

I don't speak, just look at her. At the age lines on her forehead, crows feet around her eyes. The sagging of her chin, her neck. She looks old.

Not at all like I remember.

A single tear rolls down her cheek, and despite my resolve, I look away. I never could stand to see her cry. It's one of the reasons I left, why I never went back despite the many attempts both of my parents made to get me to come home.

I couldn't after what I'd done.

The guilt only set in when they were around, and I simply couldn't live that way.

"Why'd you do it, Ivy?" she asks, and it's barely above a whisper, like she can't quite bring herself to say it. Like she doesn't want to believe what she's heard.

That's it though, all it takes for me to break.

Two point five seconds.

She's not here for me.

This isn't a mother and daughter reuniting. This is a mother seeking answers—seeking justice—for a dead daughter she can't seem to let go of.

"How could you kill your own sister?"

I just don't have the words, certainly not the ones she wants to hear. This is *her* fault, *her* actions—dad's actions—led to Erika's death, not mine.

But I don't tell her this.

She won't understand.

Instead, I stand and hang the phone back onto the wall. I nod to the corrections officer standing guard at the door and wait for him to approach. I watch my mother drop her head into her hands, I listen to her muddled cries, the long sobs with big fat tears that land in splotches on the dirty counter.

The same tears I remember shedding for so many years, while she doted on my baby sister and taught me the meaning of the word neglect.

My mother had two daughters.

And she lost one of them long before her favorite one was murdered.

It's true what they say, I guess: what goes around comes around.

So sorry to break your heart, Mother dearest.

SEX LIKE THIS

Sawyer

I used to think Ivy was in control of her life, of her own destiny. She may have been somewhat crazy, yes (okay, a lot crazy), but she knew what she was doing and why. She had an explanation, a reason, for everything.

I loved that about her, the control she had on life.

Along with her free spirit, her desire to try anything once, to think outside the box. These days? These days that take on life is kicking her ass. Part of me feels guilty; I've played a role in her legal issues, as you know, but the logical side of me says she did this to herself, regardless of the hand I played.

These are the thoughts roaming around my head as I fuck Cara for the second time today. I should really focus on what I'm doing here, stay in the moment, but my wandering mind won't settle. At least my dick is focused on the job. We're going strong doggy style so she can't see my face, how distracted I am.

I imagine that'd be an uncomfortable conversation.

Cara has surprised me, though. She's turned into a bit of a sex fiend and I love it, how easy she was to manipulate. I don't think she's all that different from the former women who've occupied my bed. If I didn't know better I'd think she was born from their combined souls.

She has the curiosity of Ivy, the drive, and unfiltered thoughts, opinions.

But she carries the same unbridled ambition and force of nature as Alisha, too, the exotic beauty.

Alarm bells go off in my head every time I welcome her, there's just something about her. She's young, off-limits. A well-educated, but sheltered mind hidden behind lingerie and closed doors when all she wants is for the world to see her.

I can't let them see her yet, I can't.

And she knows it, she knows why our relationship is taboo, why it's meant to be kept in the dark. If you ask me, that's a small price to pay for sex like this. Yeah, yeah, I realize that makes me sound ridiculously shallow, but you and I both know I don't give a shit.

I'm a man.

With needs.

I won't apologize for that.

***

In the afternoon, Caramie and I drive back to the house—my former home, soon to be Ivy's former home when I move back in and stick all her belongings in storage. It's cold of me, I know, but I'm certain she'll be taking up residency elsewhere for the foreseeable future.

I hear her first appearance didn't go as she'd hoped.

Which is why the trip to the house is on the docket for today. There's a key fob in the safe I need to retrieve, encryption codes to recapture so I can finally move this money and get Connor

Ehrens off my back.

The only real problem I seem to have now is that baby. Caramie is still caring for him while Ivy is away, which means I'm inadvertently stuck with him again. I need to find a way to remedy that issue, maybe suggest foster care or something, and make a mental note to discuss his custody with her. Today's not that day, though.

Today I have more pressing matters to tend to.

"Sawyer?" Caramie's voice interrupts my thoughts.

"You're off in La La Land..."

"Sorry, just some things on my mind."

"Anything I can help with?"

"No, beautiful, nothing for you to worry about."

"Are you looking forward to moving back home?"

"I am. It'll be nice to get out of the condo and back into the house. I've missed this place."

We pull into the drive and I enter the security code at the garage, grateful Ivy didn't get around to changing it, which is the first thing I'll take care of when we get inside.

She may be someone else's problem now, but I wouldn't put it past her to find a way to send someone over here to protect her agenda.

With the garage code changed, I head upstairs to my office, half expecting Ivy to have redecorated it, but pleased to find it untouched. I remove the picture from the wall to expose the safe, entering the code with excitement coursing throughout my veins.

This is it.

The moment I've been waiting months for.

Time to put my life back together.

But the alarm sounds when I press 'enter', a warning signal

indicating the code has been entered incorrectly.

That's weird.

Assuming I fat-fingered it, I try again, this time pressing the digits carefully, methodically.

A second warning is triggered.

I only get one more before the security company is called.

But I don't try a third time.

Because it's clear Ivy has already gotten to the safe.

And now I have a much bigger problem.

BLOOD-SUCKING LEECH

Ivy

Senior year of high school is supposed to mean something. Every teenager knows that going into it, that it'll probably be the best year of their lives and until they get married and pop out a few kids, they'll have peaked.

I refused to peak.

Not that I had much choice in the matter after the sex tape incident, but still, I had plans. I wanted more from life, a chance to stand out from the crowd, make a bigger splash than the other fish in the pond. That's why I got into acting. My art was unique, it was special. I was talented, an above average scholar with a knack for extracurriculars.

But my wholesome image had been tarnished, obliterated if I'm being honest. The new image I portrayed wasn't one I was ready to wear at first, but it grew on me in a way. Or I grew *into* it. Even though my so called "sex scandal" happened over the summer, before the start of the school year, the issue followed me into the halls. And trust me when I tell you, no one wants to walk into their Senior year of high school with a target on their back.

But that's exactly what I did.

And instead of cowering and lowering my head, I wore that target as proudly as I could, pretended the condescending looks didn't bother me, that I didn't need the acceptance of my classmates.

Everyone in school knew what I'd done, saw the evidence, teachers and faculty, included. If nothing else, they heard about it. Personally, I didn't think it was any of their business, but I was used to my opinion being moot.

Now I was a slut, an impure young woman.

The judgmental stares, the sideways glances. The scoffs, and downcast eyes as they walked past me. I was practically a local celebrity.

And the fucked up thing is, it could have happened to any one of them. I wasn't the only teenager having sex at that party, I didn't even know it was being recorded.

But none of that mattered.

The only benefit to my predicament was the newfound attention from the boys in school. A dick had been in my mouth, been inside me. Two dicks. Three. The list was growing because I allowed it to grow. The boys were finally interested in me, wanted to be with me to piss off their ex-girlfriends or write another name on their list.

And I was all for it. I was a legend amongst them, a conquest.

The game, despite my reasons for playing, was fun.

Sometimes I found myself watching it back, the video. There was something to learn from it, a desire to perfect my skills.

Erika caught me once.

She hated that I'd found a way to turn the ordeal into something positive, that it didn't (appear to) phase me as much as it once did. When she barged into my room that night, I didn't bother to pause the video, just let it play while she glared at it—and me—from the doorway.

"Can I help you?"

"Why would you let him do that to you?" she asked, her eyes revealing her adolescent ignorance. She wanted me to suffer, and I feigned the opposite just enough to piss her off more.

I shrugged, and because I wasn't sure what else to say, simply said, "I like it."

Erika folded her arms across her chest and diverted her eyes away from the screen. They kept creeping back though, just a split second here, a longer second there. She couldn't help but look, and I couldn't blame her. I looked good on screen, great even.

Her jealousy was palpable.

At sixteen now, she was still a virgin, so I understood her curiosity. She'd probably never watched porn before, maybe even thought sex was only meant for birds and bees and didn't apply to human life forms.

She shook her head, denial still prevalent in her mind. "No... there's no way anyone would like that."

I popped up, rising to my feet and jamming a finger into the power button on the monitor. "Grow up, Erika. This is how guys are, how sex works. Don't act like you have a clue about any of it."

"It's not how they are, actually," she mumbled, her face settling into a pout.

"And how would you know that? You've dated what? Two guys? *Maybe* rounded second base if I'm giving you any credit. But not a step further, right? Do you even know what third base is?"

As much as I welcomed the argument, a chance to make her look as stupid as she sounded, as stupid as she always made *me* feel, she didn't take the bait, just moved on as if I hadn't just insulted her. "Mom and Dad are still pissed."

"Yeah? Whose fault is that?"

"Don't kid yourself, Ivy. You're the one who had sex with your best friend's boyfriend."

"Why'd you do it, Erika?"

She shrugged, a smirk settling on her lips. "I guess I just felt like it."

***

Months before, Erika told our parents what she'd done and confessed to her discretion as if she was disappointed in herself when really, she was nothing but proud. Pleased. She was the superior sibling, the one in control.

She ran to Mommy and told her just where to find it. How to watch it even. That's the worst part. She could have kept the information to herself, or at the very least, asked Mom to help her take it down before it went viral. But she didn't.

She purposely waited.

In that house, I stood alone. No one was ever in my corner.

My parents, of course, were livid, not so much at Erika, but at me. Their eldest daughter was a whore. It'd be sad if it hadn't been true.

I guess some things never change.

What bothered me most, was that the video cost me the lead in the school play that year. The most important production I could've been a part of, on the last year of my high school acting career.

I wasn't even allowed to go to the show.

I knew that nothing I did would ever make my parents proud,

for them to see me as more than just another body to clothe, a mouth to feed. I was a tax deduction with living quarters on the upper level of their modest Middle America home.

Erika, on the other hand, had our parent's full interest.

Erika was a leech. A blood-sucking leech.

Not even a lobotomy could have saved her personality.

Still, they persisted. Rubbed my nose in her achievements, her success. It was worse after the tape, after I'd let them down so permanently.

"Ivy, did you hear your sister's good news?" Mom asked one night at the dinner table. I'd been pushing food around on my plate for the last ten minutes, unable to force myself to eat another casserole despite the grumbling in my stomach.

"Yep," I said without looking up.

"Isn't it wonderful? Second place in the tournament! As a sophomore!"

I dropped my fork, the metal clinking loudly against the porcelain. I didn't want to hear it anymore. I didn't give a flying fuck about my sister's tennis career. "Well, aren't you going to congratulate her?"

"Are you serious?"

"Ivy, manners," Dad chimed in.

"No! You guys missed *my* performances. All of them! *One* of you could have been there for *me*, but you always chose Erika instead. And now I didn't even get to participate this year and it's all *her* fault!"

"Your sister has a real chance at a scholarship, here, Ivy," Dad dared to say.

I shoved my plate away and get up from the table, my chair tipping and smashing against the wall, leaving a dent in the Sheetrock.

"Sit down, Ivy," Dad instructed calmly.

"Fuck you," I barked, the vein in my forehead about to burst.

Normally I wouldn't drop the 'f' bomb in front of my parents—I give myself a little credit there—but I'd had enough.

I didn't expect anyone to follow me upstairs, but it's only a few minutes later, after I've thrown the contents of my desk onto the floor and flopped myself on the bed, when I hear a soft knock on the door.

It was Dad who tried to comfort me, who took a seat on the edge of my bed and rubbed my back like I was a small child.

"What's going on, kiddo?" he finally asked.

"Nothing..."

"Doesn't seem like nothing." He nudged my shoulder, the gesture almost unexpected because of the infrequency of his affection toward me. I sat up, stunned, my expression stoic but likely leading him to the same realization.

That he never loved me enough.

We sat in silence for a moment before he spoke again, an awkward intake of breath before the words spilled out. I'm sure he was desperate for a father/daughter teaching moment, but I think it's safe to say I didn't take his advice the way it was intended.

"You know, when life throws you a curve ball, you gotta hit it. Straight out of the park. There's no time to struggle with the curve, you just gotta swing and aim for the fences."

Dad and his sports analogies. I wish I could say that one went over my head, or that I fully understood the intention behind his words, but all they did was set everything in motion for me.

I didn't want to be second best anymore.

I didn't want to strike out on the curve.

I just wanted to matter.

To exist.

It's ironic, how my father's words ended up being the ones that took his precious daughter away, but hey...curve balls, am I right?

STUPID SEAT COVERS

Ivy Rogers Diary Entry
April 12, 2005, Age 18

Literally E V E R Y T H I N G is about Erika. She's like the Marsha Brady of our house. Stupid, nerdy, ugly Erika who gets all the attention no matter what she does.

I'm so sick of this shit.

Dad bought her a car. Imagine that, huh? For her 16th yesterday. Just gave her a car like it was a rite of passage for any sixteen-year-old.

Apparently it is—for her, not me.

Because I never got a car from him when I turned sixteen. "We didn't have the money for one then, Ivy," Dad said. "Besides, you already have a car now."

She's rubbing it in my face, too. It's not brand new, no way Daddy could afford that, but it's nicer than mine—the one I bought and paid for my damn self—and that apparently gives Erika bragging rights.

He even filled up the gas tank for her, bought her some hot pink seat covers she can sit her pretentious ass on.

I want to take a shit on those stupid seat covers.

It takes a certain kind of person to do what I do, to seek revenge. I know this because I'm that certain kind of person. Hot headed. Easy to anger. Filled with grievances and grudges I can't simply ignore no matter how hard I try.

Like I told you before, I get it. I know I'm not normal in the eyes of society.

But remorse isn't really a word in my arsenal; I don't get that feeling in my gut like you do. I don't see the need to dwell on what I've done. What's done is done.

I deal with my shit.

And I deal with it the only way I know how.

Revenge.

Murder.

A new life.

That's what I need right now. A new life; a do-over. I don't think that's coming for me this time. I can't just pack up and move, run away to some foreign country and sip Mai Tais on a secluded beach with the best of them.

I *can* do something different, though.

I can shock them all, even you.

You'll see.

SHORT FUSE

Ivy

His hands make their way to my breasts and a shiver erupts in my spine. He's a gentle lover, more so than I could have imagined, and the pleasure, while welcomed, takes me a bit by surprise.

When his lips meet mine, they're possessive, silencing me and I welcome the intrusion by spreading my legs as he enters me.

"God, you feel so good." He moans against my neck and I relax into him, giving myself to him despite the alarm bells in my head.

This is wrong.

But it's so good, too.

Necessary.

"Aren't you going to arrest me, Detective?" I joke, and he smiles, the idea sparking something primal in him.

"Oh, now you like the cuffs, huh?" He winks and attaches a cuff to my wrist before securing the other end to the bed frame. I flash back to Dylan, to the sight of his body cold and lifeless, covered in blood. That morning with him was the last time I used handcuffs for sexual pleasure, when I subdued him on his own bed, in his own home, and thought of his wife as I rode his cock.

This time will be different, I tell myself.

"I know you did it, Mrs. Rogers," Detective Raylen says. It

stings, his words against my cheek, but he leaves them there like a permanent tattoo before he pulls away. "I have to take you in after this."

"No, please. You can't."

"I'm sorry, it's not my choice."

"But..."

I wake with a start, wet between my legs, anxious and longing for something that was never there after all. Something I can never have.

Detective Raylen, that's new.

How unexpected, this budding fantasy of mine. It's fitting, I suppose, considering the amount of time we've spent together lately. In such close proximity, no less.

It's still dark in my temporary cell, the lights dimmed in the common room. My bunk mate snores softly beneath me and without giving it another thought, I bring a hand to my clit and close my eyes.

This time Alisha will join us, and for the first time since they brought me here, I give myself just the release I need to keep fighting.

***

The object of this morning's wet dream sits across from Kelly Moon and me in the interview room several hours later. He's more unkempt than usual today, sporting a two-day stubble and a plaid shirt that's seen better days. Still, he looks good. Desirable. I have no doubt this man knows his way around the curves of a woman's body.

He runs a hand through his dark hair and I shift in my seat, my underwear damp as I watch the wheels in his head turn. When he finally speaks, he's laid out a legal pad, a pen resting alongside it, but he makes no attempt at note-taking.

"You were recently involved in a murder trial, were you not?" he asks.

"I was."

"The defendant in that trial seemed to believe *you* were the one who killed her husband, correct?"

"I'm aware of her claims, yes."

"And what do you make of her accusations?"

"I already testified on the matter, Detective. Perhaps you should request a copy of the transcripts? Save us both some time."

"I'd rather hear it from you."

"There's nothing to hear."

"My gut tells me otherwise."

"Sounds like you need some Tums."

He chuckles despite himself, as does Kelly, and I suppress a smile at the sight of it. He thinks he has me, that I'll cave and admit to the sins of my past. Surely, I must feel the need for repentance after all these years, right?

Wrong, next question, please.

"Tell me about your relationship with Alisha Thompson."

"There's nothing to tell, she no longer speaks to me."

"That's fine, I'm more interested in the past anyway. You two were involved romantically?"

"For a little while, yes."

"What happened?"

"She met her husband."

"And that upset you."

"That didn't sound like a question."

"It wasn't."

I see the challenge in his eyes, the desire to trap me, get me to stick my foot in my mouth. but I refuse to feed his ego. He'll need to try harder.

"Mrs. Rogers, did you kill her husband, Dylan Thompson?"

"Don't answer that," Kelly advises.

"No."

"Maybe you couldn't handle it, the idea of her with someone else."

"I was married myself you know."

"Right. Yes, your husband—*Sawyer*—he's still in the picture?"

"No."

"So, he left you, too?"

"I wouldn't say *left*."

"No? That's interesting, considering he filed for divorce recently, did he not? That must have upset you."

"You seem to think I run on a short fuse, Detective."

"Do you?"

Yes.

"No."

"How did your husband's affair with Mrs. Thompson make you feel?"

"I'm sorry, I thought this was an interrogation, not a therapy session? Why all the questions about my former relationships?"

"I'm establishing a pattern."

"Of?"

"Jealousy."

"I don't get jealous."

"No? I wonder if Joy Braverman would disagree."

"Why would—*what*? You've spoken with Joy?"

"Sure, I have."

"Why?"

"She was a close friend of yours, yes? Of your sister's?"

"She and my sister were *not* friends."

"Joy seems to think they were."

"She's lying."

"I find that hard to believe."

"Why? You seem to have no problem believing *I* would lie. She's no less capable than I am."

"Again, I'm establishing a pattern here."

"You haven't caught me in a single lie."

"Perhaps I have."

"What makes you so sure?"

He slides a sheet of paper across the table. Already I recognize it, I know what it is, what the words are and what sentences they make up.

It's a photocopy, but it holds the integrity of the original just the same.

Ivy Rogers Diary Entry
Friday, August 4, 2006

I did it.

I killed my sister today.

I killed her and the only thing I feel is relief.

She's finally gone.

I have to call Joy. If I call her, she'll come to me. She'll hold me while I cry.

She'll forgive me. Who doesn't forgive someone after their little sister dies so tragically?

She has to.

Because I don't want to think about what happens if she doesn't.

SNAPPED

Ivy

Evidence is a funny thing, isn't it?

To think that we leave so many tiny traces of ourselves behind is kinda scary. But that's what we do; our DNA is everywhere, whether we leave it on purpose or not. A signature, if you will.

But somehow, in my case, they didn't need DNA to prove anything. They didn't need blood, or fibers, or hair, or even a verbal confession.

I'd left them something much more damaging.

I don't remember writing the diary entry. Maybe I blocked it out, wanted to believe that I didn't do it, that I couldn't have possibly done something so stupid.

But it's a smoking gun.

A bullet that's reached its intended target.

Ivy Rogers Diary Entry
Friday, August 4, 2006

She stole my best friend.

Right from under my nose. I've lost her and she seems to have gone running straight to Erika. She had to know how much that would piss me off, right? Who the hell does she think she is?

Am I that *replaceable?*

We had plans, Joy and I. For life, the rest of high school, college. And now, all because I kissed her and ruined everything, she's nothing more than a stranger. A memory of the past.

I'm so fucking stupid.

I festered for hours, wallowed in nothing but my own pity, at the thought of my best friend and my only sister replacing *me* as easily as a weathered pair of sneakers.

I'm the chewed up gum stuck to the sole at the bottom.

Joy's car trolled down the street and into our driveway slowly, like she wanted to scope out the place to make sure I wasn't there before committing to a parking spot. I watched from the shadowy bowels of the garage, my diary and pen in my lap as they pulled into the driveway and cut the engine.

I closed my diary and tucked it safely into the pocket of Dad's golf bag, it wasn't like he used it anymore, and stuffed the heavy tool behind my back, out of sight and into the pocket of my jeans before covering it with my shirt.

My heart ached at the reminder that I'd lost her, that she wasn't my best friend anymore. And now she was off gallivanting with my little sister, a girl she couldn't stand any more than I could growing up. A girl who put us in this predicament.

I've been telling her what she's like for years, how she'll do anything to protect herself. I was sure it was only a matter of time before she'd screw Joy over, too. I needed to help her, get her away from my sister.

The urge to pull her aside and talk to her was strong. To tell her again that I'm sorry, that I never meant to hurt her. But she didn't step out of the car, just used the crank to roll down her window and offer a tentative wave as Erika unfolded from the passenger seat.

Even that hurt, the site of her looking so small, so afraid. I'd done nothing to give the impression that I was someone to fear, so the display took me by surprise.

"I don't bite, you know," I mumbled.

She pretended not to hear me, like my words were lost in the wind. I hated what we'd become: strangers in a familiar world.

"Oh, get over yourself!" Erika huffed with a flip of her hair. She slammed the car door behind her, slinging her purse over her shoulder and walking toward me. "Maybe you should've kept your legs closed," she whispered, shoving me in the shoulder before heading to the front door of the house.

I wanted to tackle her, shove her face into the concrete and make her bleed.

But I couldn't.

Not in front of Joy.

But Joy was finished with the conversation, I could tell. She rolled up her window, punctuating the act with a click of the automatic door lock. She waved goodbye—to Erika—and retreated down the driveway.

I huffed, muffling a scream, and stomped into the house and up to my room. I couldn't believe she had dismissed me like that.

And I didn't know what I'd done to instill such fear in her, it wasn't like my queerness was contagious and all I did was try to kiss her. There's no threat here.

Why can't she see that?

***

With the house quiet and Mom and Dad out for the night, I retrieved the tool from my desk and sneaked outside through the back door of garage. To Erika's precious car parked on the street in front of mine.

It wouldn't be long now, before Erika emerged from her bedroom, gothed out in a mini skirt and black eyeliner, ready to attend a kegger at Kayla Fox's place.

Little did she know, she wouldn't be attending the party after all.

"You need Jesus, Ivy," she'd said to me earlier.

The last words my sister ever spoke to me, and I can't say she was wrong, but they're not words I dwell on. They certainly don't keep my up at night.

Our poor parents, huh?

I suppose I had a good run; sixteen years is a long time to get away with murder these days if you think about it. In some ways, I always knew this day would come. Welcomed it even.

I definitely wasn't expecting it yet, but shit happens.

All I can do now is keep my mouth shut.

Deny everything.

Although that didn't work out so well for Alisha, now did it?

***

Ivy Rogers Diary Entry
Friday, August 4, 2006
(continued)

I snapped.

It was bound to happen sooner or later.

Honestly, I'm surprised I was able to hold out this long.

I doubt she saw it coming, that she had any sense I was so close to losing it. It's unfortunate, really. She could have saved herself. Or tried to, but I doubt it would have mattered.

My mind was made up.

I looked down at my sister's battered body, at the thick stream of blood making its way through the cracks in the dirt, the tilt of her head unnaturally wedged in the ground, her leg folded beneath her. The jarring image does nothing but bring a smile to my face.

How lucky for me that she chose today, of all days, not to wear a seatbelt.

This couldn't have worked out any better.

I pushed to my feet and turned toward the vehicle a good twenty feet from the body, taking in what remained of the wreckage. Smoke from the engine polluted the air in dark plumes, glass littered in chunky shards on the ground around the base of the tree it struck. It leaned to the left now, its massive trunk cracked at the base, the root unearthed.

Yet, the tree remained standing, erect and alive to see another day.

I couldn't say the same for Erika.

A head wound like that? Come on. Surely, she must've died on impact.

Such a shame, too.

Mom and Dad will be so heartbroken.

SEVENTEEN

Ivy

It's eerily quiet here.

I kinda thought it would be louder, in the county jail, but it seems the loudest thing in the room are my thoughts, all-encompassing and intrusive. There's a lot of time to think in here, to reflect, and I don't know what to make of that. I wonder how much they know, how much they think they can prove without any sort of confession on my end.

I'll go down swinging though, it's what I do.

I wonder if Sawyer knows I'm here, and how baby Dylan is doing with Caramie. I haven't called home yet, it's not like I can talk to a baby, and I don't really have anything to say to Cara anyway. She can make do without me until all this blows over.

She'll be fine.

Besides, I have a lot on my mind right now, especially today. I can't help but relive everything that's happened.

Erika was weak, in too deep with no way to paddle ashore. She thought she could take me on, but she was wrong. She should have been stronger, smarter. Her mistakes cost her everything.

If she would have just stayed out of it, minded her own

business, left me alone. Things could have ended so differently for her. For us.

I remember how her face had changed and never went back to normal, like it was locked in forever. Her eyes bulged, her lips drooped. Her hair slick with blood. I cradled her head in my arms for just a moment.

Sometimes I wonder if she knew, if she had that moment of clarity.

I'll never know, but I like to think she did.

But it's Dylan's death that's occupying my mind right now, Alisha's subsequent trial and conviction. I keep trying to forget, to move on and stop fantasizing about everyone, but I can't. *Something* in me knows what I've done is morbid and wrong.

It's murder.

Murder is illegal.

But it never seems to matter how many times I pretend I didn't do these things, that I didn't kill these people. It just keeps coming back to me, like a perpetual *Lifetime* movie on repeat. I can't unsee it.

I can't un-smell it.

The flashes of red.

Wet.

Thick.

One.

The blood that splays on the wall behind me, on the ceiling, on my clothes. It drips in globs onto the carpet, sure to leave one hell of a stain when all is said and done.

My vision blurs, but still I see red splotches.

I can't stop seeing red.

Two.

He did this to himself.

No, *she* did this to him.

She did this to us.

They did it to each other.

Three.

To me, to Sawyer.

Why didn't she love me?

Four.

She lied.

They both lied, we all did. It's in our nature, I guess, in our need for self preservation and repentance. But how did it come to this? How did we get here?

Five.

"Why can't you be more responsible like Erika?"

Where's your precious Erika now, Mom?

Six.

My head throbs with tension, the muscles in my neck stiff and sore, but I can't stop now. I can't put this knife down, it just keeps going in and out of his body.

Seven.

I'll need to pack up the car.

She'll come with me, she has to.

What just dripped down my thigh? When did I have sex?

Eight.

My arm is so sore, the muscles tight, the veins bulging, but I keep stabbing because I don't know how to stop and for some reason, this feels really good right now.

I see their faces: Alisha's, Sawyers. I see the three of us together, happy.

Before he took that away from us.

Before he stole her for himself.

Nine.

Why would he do that?

He could've been a part of it, we would have let him in. Sawyer may be stubborn, but he didn't want to lose Alisha any more than I did. We could have found a way to make it all work.

A foursome.

Fun.

Ten.

No, not fun.

Stressful.

Stupid.

Certainly ridiculous.

Wishful thinking?

Eleven.

Definitely wishful thinking.

Ugh.

What happens now?

Twelve.

Why the fuck is it so hot in here?

I need some air. Some cool—no, *cold*—air. To breathe.

I feel like I've just run a marathon.

I don't even like running.

Thirteen.

Alisha loves running.

That's where she is right now, running.

I wonder if she gets that runner's high everyone always talks about.

Is it anything like actually *being* high?

Fourteen.

I doubt it.

Nothing beats that.

Fifteen.

Everything hurts.

Literally. Everything.

My arm...

I'm so week, I could collapse.

I *actually* think I'm about to collapse.

I can't let that happen.

Just a bit more now...please.

Sixteen.

It's over, this pain. It's time for her to bear the brunt of it now.

I've carried this weight for us long enough.

Seventeen.

This is overkill, I know that. It didn't have to be this bad, this many stab wounds.

What a fucking mess.

I think I'm gonna puke.

Why did I stab him so many times?

I look down at the body. He's stopped breathing, I don't know when, but there's no way he could live through this.

There's so much blood.

Seventeen.

That's when everything changed, that moment I've been searching for.

The first time I saw red and never looked back. The age I was when my sister took her last breath, when I reached my breaking point and couldn't take it anymore.

See, this is all Erika's fault.

It's *always* Erika's fault.

THE GOOD DAUGHTER

Ivy

I could lie and say I never meant to hurt my sister.

I could do that.

But what's the point? How would that help? The simple answer is that it wouldn't. My intentions were impure, unnatural. Harmful. Lying won't change that. It won't bring her back (not that I want to), and it sure as shit won't fix things with my parents (not that I want to do that either).

But it's important for me to play the role of a lifetime here, to act the part. Pretend. Detective Raylen needs to think I love my parents, that I miss them dearly and would like nothing more than to welcome them back into my life. I need a poor me, a hail Mary.

My mother used to call me her little peanut. She'd put one of those plastic barrettes in my hair, right at the tippy-top of my head, and those wispy ends would stick straight up just like Pebbles in *The Flintstones.* She doted on me. Loved me. Went out of her way to make me giggle, to play, and snuggle up with me to watch my favorite cartoons even though she had a million better things to do than watch children's shows.

She did all those things, she loved me and I felt that love, that admiration.

We lost that somewhere. It was as if it dissipated as quickly as it had come.

But yes, there was a time before all this when things were fine, when I could be around my mother and not let her suck the life out of me. Now I have a hard time remembering those days.

If I were to guess, to try to point my finger at a target and say exclusively that *this* is when it all went to shit, that target would harbor the face of my newborn baby sister right smack dab in the center of it.

Erika ruined everything.

From the moment she was born.

She was the new and improved epicenter of my mother's world, the one and only concern on her mind, and Dad simply followed her in blind ignorance. Almost like he didn't know any better.

It was like they'd forgotten they had another daughter.

They'd replaced me, and as if overnight I went from being their everything to a full time babysitter for the sister I never wanted. I was the silent helper, the tiny tot whose sole purpose was to remind her parents that not all children are created equal.

My new purpose was that of a caregiver, the toddler version of a handy helper.

Ivy, grab Momma a diaper, will you?

Ivy, hand Momma that bottle.

The night it happened, I simply lost the will to fight it anymore. I wanted her dead, since the moment I first laid eyes on her. Seventeen years was a long time to wait. A long time to plot and fantasize, to pretend.

I was done pretending.

Ivy, give your Dad a break and take out the trash.

Ivy, don't look at your little sister like that.

Ivy, stop pestering me while I'm holding the baby.

Ivy, grow up!

In fact, I was proud of myself for holding out, that I hadn't killed her the first time I'd thought of it, or the second, the third...I gave Erika plenty of chances to do better. To not suck, to help me show Mom and Dad that I wasn't the tyrant they thought I was.

Instead she did the opposite.

Ivy, why can't you be more like your sister?

She pitted them against me, showed them all the ways I was a disappointment. She was the good daughter, the one they *wanted* around, the one they'd do anything for.

To be honest, it was harder pretending to be sad about my sister's *accidental death* than it was to kill her. My parents were beside themselves, the community shaken.

She was so young, they'd say. *Her whole life ahead of her.*

Even in death, Erika had everyone's attention.

That's why I left.

Every time I saw my sister's face in pictures all I could think about was other ways to kill her. Less humane ways. But instead, I put on a brave face and did what I could to console my poor, sad, parents through the loss of their favorite daughter. And then once the dust settled, I would resume my role as the only child and everything would be just like it was before Erika was born.

She'd be erased faster than a bad idea.

And I'd be the good daughter again.

And that's really the best way I can think to describe the way I feel anytime someone wrongs me; it never goes away really, this desire to control things. First it was Erika, my parents. Then Dylan, Alisha.

I wonder who will be next?

I'M FINE

Sawyer

Marriage isn't for everyone.

I've learned this the hard way, but I suppose all that matters is that I've learned it. Life's greatest lessons are often learned through trial and error.

I don't plan to do this again, not that I've shared that fact with anyone other than you. But I'm in a predicament, because I see a spark in Caramie's eyes whenever we're together. I know the way she looks at me, I recognize the longing in her eyes. Like she knows I'm her future. It won't be easy letting her down, but I'll have to eventually, when the time is right and I no longer need her anymore.

I certainly can't put myself through this a second time; best to love and let go if you ask me.

This divorce has hit me harder than I thought it would. I was doing pretty well, keeping my heart and mind at bay, but at this point, I need closure. I need to see Ivy, to be with my wife one last time before she isn't my wife anymore.

So, that's why I'm going, why I'm headed to the county jail to see her.

I hadn't planned to, of course I hadn't, but somehow I'm

behind the wheel and headed in that direction. She's like a force of nature the way she manages to dictate my actions even when she's not around.

This is the last time, though.

After today, we're through.

I'll make sure of it.

***

Seeing her in the jumpsuit brings images of Alisha straight to the forefront. Ivy looks downright helpless in the faded orange getup, behind the glass where I can't even touch her, feel the warmth of her hand. Like she's on display at a museum.

I didn't expect to be separated by a partition.

The moment is brief, but I feel it, the guilt.

I put her here.

I did this to her.

The admission rests on my tongue, ready to take the leap from my mouth to her ears despite my will to stop it.

But I do, I stop it because there's no other way.

I know what kind of damage Ivy could do with that kind of information.

Confinement within these walls won't stop her once she's set her mind to something, and the last thing I want to do is give her more ammunition.

No, I need her behind this barrier.

This is where she belongs.

"I miss you," she says into the phone, and I know my wife is a liar, but every other part of me knows she means it, she misses me and she can't help herself any more than I can. I want to say it back, because it's true, but I don't.

I can't.

"How are you holding up in there?" I ask instead.

"I'm fine."

"Ah, the classic, *I'm fine.*"

"Don't patronize me, Sawyer."

"I'm sorry. Just wasn't sure what to say."

"What are you doing here?"

"I wanted to see you. Make sure you're all right." And I did, it's true. Seeing her like this though, this isn't what I had in mind.

No makeup.

Hair piled like a bird's nest on top of her head.

This isn't my wife.

"Ah, so sweet of you," she says, and the sarcasm isn't lost on me. I hear it, feel it like tension at the end of an anchor.

"I'm moving back into the house," I admit, and her eyes light up. Her lips form a smile, but it's not the Ivy I remember. This Ivy is filled with hope, needy.

"You're waiting for me?"

"No, Ivy."

"Then you have no reason to be there." Her smile fades as quickly as it came, and she moves to stand, but I place a hand on the counter to settle her back down.

"It's my home."

"It was *our* home," she snaps. Tears well in the corners of her eyes, and it's almost heartbreaking to watch.

Almost.

"Not anymore."

"Why are you doing this?"

"I've drawn up a settlement agreement. There's some money set aside for you. When the divorce goes through, it'll be there for you. I'll have the accountant make monthly deposits to your accounts, keep up with your bills."

She shrinks against the seat, the plastic squeaking. "I guess you win then." She shrugs, and I can't tell if she's admitting defeat or demonstrating compliance. Either way, I take it. I didn't come here to argue.

"I think we have different definitions of winning," I say.

"What about Caramie? And Dylan? They live there now, you know. In the house. You're really going to put them out on the street?"

This is it. The moment I dreaded when I decided I was coming here today. Suddenly my throat feels dry; apparently my conscience decided to join me for the trip.

"Sawyer?"

"Look, Ivy, Caramie and the kid will be fine. They're taken care of."

"What do you mean they're taken care of?"

"We're ah...together. Cara and me."

Her face falls, and I see the fear in her eyes, sense the pain in her chest. I know I've hurt her enough already; this is just icing on the cake.

But she was going to find out sooner or later.

"How—*how* could you do this to me? You didn't want that baby to begin with!"

"No, I suppose I didn't. Things change I guess."

And it's cowardly, I know, but I've said what I needed to say, delivered the news that I came here to deliver. "I loved you, Ivy."

I hang the phone on wall, press my hand on the partition as Ivy slams her end of the line onto the counter. She beats her fits into the Plexiglass as she screams.

As the guards apprehend her, cuff her, and drag her out of

the room.

I watch my wife disappear behind the locked door.

And I let her take my heart right along with her.

THE DARKNESS WINS

Ivy

Life is awkward, it's unfair.

Everybody lives and everybody dies.

Some us lie down and take it, while others—like me—do something about it. We live life to the fullest, no matter the consequences.

It's human nature really.

A never-ending cycle that we hope to go through with the support of family, of friends. I, however, am more alone than I ever thought.

There's a darkness in me, mean bones, as Mom used to say. And when that darkness takes over it's all encompassing. The light is switched off. I'm overcome with emotions beyond my control.

But can you really fear what you can't see? The unknown? All the tiny monsters lurking in the corner.

I like to think there's something more out there, in that darkness. A higher power, maybe. Who knows? Maybe I'm wrong and just overthinking this.

All I know is that the light doesn't always come back.

Sometimes the darkness wins.

And once again, I'm a lone bird in the sky, soaring against the blue. I stand out, make my presence known without even trying.

Free.

I plead guilty, I should probably mention that. Go ahead and act surprised, I know you want to.

But despite my lawyer's advice, despite the minuscule amount of evidence against me, I took the plea deal. I'll be an inmate for the next twenty-five years. I could be out with good behavior in much less, not that I'm likely to behave.

I know it's crazy, but I'm confident in my decision; standing by it proudly just as I did the day I watched my sister drive off down the street with her brake lines severed.

There's no reward without the risk, right?

Detective Raylen is under the impression I've plead guilty simply because I *feel* guilty, that I regret what I've done, who I've hurt in the process. It's good to let him think that for now, but I don't regret anything.

Not even a little bit.

That's not why I took the plea deal, though, why I waived my right to a fair and speedy trial, my day in court. I give a shit about a lot of things, but the opinion of this detective is not one of them. The truth is, avoiding a trial, taking it on the chin for a crime I'm well aware I committed, really is just a matter of self preservation. A means to an end, sure, but a rather humane one at that.

If you haven't figured it out yet, pleading guilty was the only way to make sure I'm never tied to Dylan's murder. He was onto me, Raylen, and I wasn't about to peel back the curtain when the show had already started, you know?

Surely, they won't reopen the investigation on Dylan's murder when the only two suspects are already behind bars, especially given our sentences.

So, this is it.

A moment of truth, a homecoming of sorts.

I'm off to see my girl.

HELLO, LISHA

Alisha

"Hey, Barbie," Ronnie coos. She takes a seat next to me at the chow table and chomps into her sandwich, chewing it wildly, with her mouth wide open like a cow in a pasture. A smirk plays on her lips as if the dry bologna sandwich she's scarfing down actually tastes good. I turn the page in the book I'm skimming and suppress the urge to moo. I'm fairly certain she'll take it as an insult to her build instead of her obnoxious chewing habits.

I'm not in the mood for Ronnie's shit today.

I'm never in the mood for anyone's shit, really.

And I hate myself for it, but I catch myself scanning the room for Tiffany. I wish I didn't look forward to her joining us, but I'm human, so sometimes the attention feels good.

It's been an interesting first year here at Smithson, starting with the borrowed use of the shiv that helped me take out Officer Marshall. I've been on edge ever since, somewhat of a bitch even.

Tiffany's, that is.

I spot her in the chow line, nearly through with a full tray, and release a sigh of relief.

While it was never my intention to attach myself to Tiffany's hip, she's here and she keeps me off the radar so for now, I'm playing nice, behaving. It's safe to say I eventually gave her the lead and let her drag me around with it.

I'm not sure how much longer it'll last, but I take advantage of it for now, her protection and what it affords me.

I take a bite of my own bologna sandwich, the Wonder bread sticking to the roof of my mouth before it descends down my throat in a clump. Food is no longer a vice for me, but rather a means of survival. A necessary component to get through the day.

Not that I wouldn't kill for a plate of Lasagna Classico.

But I need the distraction today. My mind is elsewhere, my thoughts a randomized cluster of apprehension.

I saw her face on the news this morning, during rec hour.

She was right there, front and center, her mug shot like a lackluster glamour shot, but it was her. I'd know that mole anywhere, that dead expression in her eyes.

Suburbanite pleads guilty to sister's sixteen-year long unsolved murder.

I'd give it less thought if I could, but alarm bells have been ringing in my head since the broadcast, since the admission of guilt I hadn't seen coming.

She didn't try to fight it.

As if by design.

I have a pretty good idea where she's heading, too, as I'm sure you do.

In retrospect, I should have done things differently. I should have looked out for myself, for Dylan. Maybe even for Sawyer if I'm being honest.

I know that now.

But I can't change the past any more than I can hop the fence and skip-to-my-lou out of here. I don't get a do over. All I can do is go on living, eyes forward, with a can-do attitude—or some shit like that. There's not much else to do here, and right now my only goal is to get through today, to muster through work assignments so I can head back to my cell where I belong.

I close my book, one of the newer releases Chris sent me last week. I'm grateful for the distraction it provides but can't seem to focus on the words on the page, especially with Ronnie assaulting her food across the table. I pick up the trash around me and lock eyes with Tiffany. She smiles as she makes her way to our table. Lunch will only go another ten minutes, but it's still ten minutes I'm not in the mood for.

Not today.

"Where you off to, playmate?" she teases, her smile fading.

I force one in response, an attempt to ease her trepidation I suppose, but it's weak and doesn't do the trick. She sees right through it.

"What's wrong?" she asks, setting her tray down on the table but not taking a seat. Ronnie stares up at her, and I savor the pregnant pause in her chewing.

"I'm not feeling the greatest," I lie, bringing a pointer finger to my head. "A bit of a headache creeping in."

"No time for headaches," she says, stepping closer. She snakes a possessive arm around my waist and gives my hip a squeeze. "There's a new girl coming in."

"Why do I care?"

"Rumor has it, she's a friend of yours."

My heart drops, the tension in my body suddenly stiff and intrusive. I smell her before I even turn around, my senses somehow heightened just because we're in the same room. "Hello, Lisha," I hear.

I turn, so slowly I turn, certain I'm about to pass out. I didn't think she'd get here so soon.

Oh, but she is.

Right there in perfect porcelain flesh, no more than ten feet away, wearing the proverbial orange jumpsuit, the one with DOC in big black letters on the back of it that tells me she's fresh out of intake.

Tiffany takes a step forward before I manage to move my feet. They're frozen to the ground; the ice always takes a minute to thaw when Ivy walks into a room.

"Oh, this is going to be fun," Tiffany says, drinking her in, a wide smile taking over her face.

Ivy smiles, too, and it reaches her eyes, bright and beaming.

For some reason, I smile back.

And then all I hear is music.

Because now I finally know how I'll kill her.

AYE, ME LUCKY CHARMS

Sawyer

Her face is on the front page.

Ivy really is a looker, even in a DOC jumpsuit. But what makes me smile is seeing both of them together, she and Alisha; my girls. The spotlight always did them best, I should know. Ivy's sentencing has stirred up some renewed interest in Alisha's case. The media has exposed their history, they know their story now. It made sense to share their unexpected reunion with the public.

Their faces are side by side on the front page, the headline sure to captivate even an outsider.

Former lovers reunited at Smithson.

I set the newspaper on the counter and grab a box of cereal from the cabinet—Lucky Charms today, because well, I'm feeling kinda lucky. My wife is finally off to prison, I'm moving back into my house—where my mistress already lives with my wife's illegitimate son—and I no longer have to worry about her taking me to the cleaners.

The once damning evidence against me has been securely restored, out of reach to anyone but me. My ties to the Ehrens-Havenbrook Corporation will remain unnoticed.

I even found the missing account codes from the safe.

Life really is looking up for Sawyer Rogers, huh?

I scoop another bite of cereal into my mouth, the marshmallows squishy and slimy and reminding me of my childhood. I usually prefer a fancier breakfast spread, but no one's here to cook for me this morning and I just don't have the time to do it myself. It's fine, just a quick bowl before I shower and head to the office.

It'll be busy today, being my last...day in the office...before I move back. Home, that is. Sorry, not sure...why.

Wow, it's odd, the sensation swimming in my head right now.

Foggy...

A bit hazy...

I guess that's just a synonym for fog, though, huh?

Sorry, my mind is a little out of it right now.

Like I'm swimming under water...everything sounds far away.

It's bright in here...

Almost too bright all of a sudden.

Wow, my vision is seriously fucked up.

I can't even read the words on the cereal box, and *oh my fucking god*, what the hell is going on?

I'm warm, then suddenly freezing.

And now...I...can't...

...breathe, for...some...reason.

It happens then, the end of my life. How unexpected it was, too. I can't help but wonder if Dylan felt the same way when his life was cut short. Keeling over into a bowl of soggy cereal wasn't my ideal way to go out—it's really not very manly, I know—but I guess it beats seventeen stab wounds to the chest.

I always knew she'd come for me.

A bird certainly can't fly without its wings.

But what's most surprising, what I don't expect, is that it's not Ivy's face I see in that last moment, it's not my estranged wife who takes a predatory step into the room as I suck the last breath of air I'll ever take into my lungs.

It's Caramie's.

And she doesn't look even the least bit concerned.

Where the hell did I go wrong?

WHO WILL BE HER LOVER?

Alisha

Things have a funny way of working themselves out, don't they? For instance, I've been convicted of murder (as you know), but I didn't commit murder until I ended up in this place, in this prison. It's a crime I must admit, I didn't think I was capable of.

Anywhere outside of here, one might be able to argue self-defense.

But nobody believes a convicted criminal. Hell, few believe any woman who'd take their clothes off for money. I was doomed from the start, blacklisted. And that's fine, I'm okay with that now.

The thing is, a handful of other women came forward with complaints about our fallen CO's conduct after I killed him. I think they hoped it would lessen my sentence, maybe help in some way.

It didn't.

Not when you kill a cop in cold blood; there's no leniency on a charge like that, even if he *was* a predatory psychopath. It turns out, the word of a few incarcerated inmates doesn't hold strong against a fallen officer, especially without proof.

But it's okay, really. I knew I'd be stuck here for the rest of my life even before I did it. Maybe that's *why* I was able to, why it felt right. I couldn't live like that, in fear, every day for the rest of my life. So, no, killing Officer Marshall isn't the heaviest regret I carry around with me.

Sometimes it makes me feel better knowing the other women who came forward can rest easy though. That their stories were heard, even if not believed by those in power.

For me? It brings comfort. It wasn't easy to hear what they'd been through.

But Caramie's hit me the hardest.

She, unlike the rest of us, had to live with that monster. Three years she stood beside him before he met his current wife (now widow), blind to the fact that there were others, that his rein didn't exist solely behind closed doors.

Until the news broke: Officer Joshua Marshall had been murdered by an inmate.

She came to thank me.

I'd spent two months in solitary confinement before that, locked alone with my thoughts, withering away to nearly nothing, questioning my decision and whether it was as necessary as it felt at the time.

It was her voice that made it worth it, her story.

Not that it's mine to tell, I suppose I'll leave that up to her.

Maybe she'll tell it to you one day.

AN EASY TEN MILLION

Caramie

The wire transfer will hit my account before I make it out the door of Sawyer's apartment. I know I need to move quickly, get the hell out of here before anyone sees me, but still I take a moment. Breathe in a deep sigh of relief, exhale it back out.

I did it.

I'm fucking rich.

Man, that was a rush. I really wasn't sure I could pull it off, that I could take him down in time, but here I go. I'm in the car now, baby Dylan strapped into his car seat behind me. We're headed for the freeway, the open road, and onto bigger and better things.

"You excited for our new adventure, Dyl?"

This was such a big job, one I've stressed over since the moment she asked for my help. She had faith in me, though, she did. She saw something in me, and it's a relief to know it's all working out. She'll be so pleased with the results, I know she will.

I owe her *everything.*

After all, she saved *my* life, the least I could do was save her son.

TO BE CONTINUED...

ACKNOWLEDGMENTS

I learned something new while writing this book: there's a whole new kind of pressure that comes with writing a series. This was hella stressful!

I'm already anticipating *your* first question though...*but Shannon, when do we get book three? I need to know what happens next!*

Soon, grasshopper, soon.

I'd like to share something with you; a little history behind a main character in the book. Back when I was a single momma, my kids and I spent four years living in a townhouse on Ivy Ridge Lane. We were blessed with the most amazing neighbor, Vicki, who had the kindest heart and the only two little dogs in the world that my son liked at the time. Vicki was an avid reader, incredibly supportive of my writing, and was so excited to read my debut novel, *My Only Sunshine*; she couldn't wait to get her hands on a copy and never missed an opportunity to tell me. Sadly, Vicki passed away in 2020, just four months before the book was published. I chose Ivy's name in honor of my dear friend and neighbor from Ivy Ridge Lane. I know she would have loved her level of crazy, and been first in line for my book signings. This book is dedicated to her, and I hope it would've made her proud.

And now, an honest truth: I originally planned to leave you hanging and not write this sequel right away. I know, I know, that's not very nice of me, but luckily, when I finished writing *Wouldn't You Love to Love Her* I ended up rolling right into this one. I had a few ideas of where the book was going to go and just wanted to get them down on the page, a general summary if you will, so I didn't forget. Those "notes" turned into ten entire chapters and almost 20,000 words within just a handful of days, so I ran with it and now here we are. I didn't think Ivy's voice would come to me so naturally, but I'm grateful—as I'm sure *you* are—that it did.

In fact, I may have enjoyed writing Ivy's story even more than I enjoyed writing Alisha's. That was unexpected, but some days I like this book more than WYLTLH. It feels like I'm picking a favorite child, but please don't judge me for it.

The Smithson Women's Penitentiary is a completely fictional prison set on some random farmland in Minnesota. I teetered with using a real prison, but I didn't feel comfortable doing that without touring a facility and to be honest, I have absolutely no desire to do that. All my prison-related research took place behind a computer screen, thank you very much (that said, any and all mistakes are my own!)

And on that note, I have several people I'd like to thank.

To my husband, Taylor, and my kids who are growing up much too quickly for my liking: thank you for allowing me the time and space necessary to work on my craft.

To my talented editor, Keizha Ferrell of Librum Artis Editorial Services: I'll sing your praises every single day. Thank you for all you do to help bring my stories to life. Truly. It's incredibly difficult to find a reliable editor and I understand how lucky I am to have snagged you. I already look forward to partnering with you on book three!

To my Jump Street Team: Wow! You guys have really hit it hard with this series, and I am SO grateful! Your support of my books is appreciated beyond words.

Thank you to the bookstagram community for their continued support and encouragement! Several of you managed to snake your way into this book and for that, you're welcome.I hope you enjoyed seeing your names in print, whether you approved of your character or not, it was fun finding ways to incorporate you into this series! Erika @erikalaceyreads, Sawyer Cole @colesbooknook, Alisha @alishareadsgoodbooks, Caramie @memyshelfandwine, Cristina @frostyourshelf, Krissy @books_and_biceps9155, Sebastian @seb.reads, Chris @analyzedbychris, Bethany @bethanyburiedinbooks, and Kelly @dearbooks_iloveyou (you're a lifesaver for helping me out with that court scene, by the way).

A special thank you to Erika Lacey for beta reading my early drafts and talking through the intricacies of the plot with me! Your notes, suggestions, and endless support are so greatly appreciated!

Chris, I'll never forget our conversation when I first shared my ideas about the plot; your reaction was priceless, and the motivation I desperately needed to get this one off the ground!

Thank you to Diana Rose @angelsmomreads for coining the phrase "deceptively charming sociopath" and letting me use it in the book! It fits this series so perfectly, and I fell in love with it right away!

And lastly, to YOU, dear reader. Whether you loved this book, liked it only a little, or completely hated it, thank you so much for picking it up and giving it a read.

Until next time...

The Crimes of Passion series continues!

The best of two worlds collide in the conclusion of this intensely provocative and addicting psychological thriller series. Full of steam *and* scream, seduction, and deception, the *Crimes of Passion* series is fast-paced, witty, and sure to leave readers on the edge of their seats.

Next in Series Coming Soon:

Who Will Be Her Lover

About the Author

Shannon Jump is an avid reader and writer of multiple genres, with a passion for storytelling. She refuses to start the day without the perfect cup of coffee, is a die-hard Minnesota Twins baseball fan and Food Network junkie. She lives in small-town Minnesota with her husband and two teenage kids.

You can connect with me on:

https://www.shannonjumpwritesbooks.com

Also by Shannon Jump

WOULDN'T YOU LOVE TO LOVE HER
Crimes of Passion Series Book 1

Life has never been easy for the strikingly beautiful Alisha Thompson.

As an admitted sex addict and adult webcam performer, Alisha's highly troubled past—a childhood riddled with abandonment and neglect that's left her nearly void of emotions—comes back to haunt her. When her husband, Dylan, ends up dead, she's found wide-eyed in the corner of the room, the murder weapon tightly gripped in her hand.

And covered in blood.

The evidence against her is compelling. Now incarcerated, she awaits trial for the brutal murder, and everyone—including her high stakes attorney—seems to doubt her innocence.

The Minnesota case takes the media by storm, and as a lifelong loner, Alisha knows she has no one to turn to. Her life suspended, she spends the long days in prison keeping the other inmates at arm's length, desperate to evade a life sentence.

But prison brings its own challenges.

And when an unexpected face from her past shows up in the courtroom, will Alisha be out for justice? Or revenge?

Intensely provocative and addicting, *Wouldn't You Love to Love Her* is a disturbing psychological thriller that will keep readers guessing until the very last page.

EVEN THOUGH IT'S BREAKING

Allie Mason has it all: a handsome and doting boyfriend, a great career as an editor for an independent publisher, and a reliable best friend who keeps her on her toes. Coupled with her girl-next-door looks, Allie is a textbook definition of happy everything.

Until one night, she's stripped of it all.

Allie is attacked in her home, badly beaten and raped—with no memory of the traumatizing events that took place that night.

As Allie works to uncover the truth, she's left with more questions than answers—and forced to make an unimaginable decision.

With her attacker still at large, Allie is gripped by fear—and the growing sensation that someone has been following her.

That they may be out there...watching.

Waiting.

MY ONLY SUNSHINE

"My story is like that of many before me. I am a victim of domestic abuse and marital rape, a battered woman. I fell in love with a tall, dark and handsome man; a self-proclaimed bad boy with an unexpected and worsening drug problem. I was blind to his true colors when I said my vows and I feared there was no turning back."

Set in a small town in Minnesota and spanning over twenty years, Brynn Reeves navigates through an abusive marriage, motherhood, and friendship while coming to terms with the unexpected path her life has taken. Based loosely on true events, *My Only Sunshine* is a story of love, determination, and strength, filled with raw emotion and kick-you-in-the-gut heartbreak.

They said until death do them part; will Brynn find the strength to get out before it's too late?

Made in the USA
Middletown, DE
17 June 2022